SAVAGE THINGS

CALLIE HART

CHAOS & RUIN

BOOK TWO

ONE

Mason

A bird flew into the window of the house when I was a kid. I can't remember what kind of bird it was. Its wings were brown, golden in places, and the tips of its feathers were tinged with a subtle blue that could only be seen at a certain angle when the light caught at them. The bird was broken. Its tiny chest rose and fell rapidly, its beak gaping open, its black eyes filled with fear. My father, high as fuck, just like always, had picked it up and placed it into my hands. I was seven years old, and he told me to wring its neck.

"Look at it, boy. It's done. Ain't no point in bringin' it inside and having it shit all over the house."

I'll still never know why he was so concerned about the tiny, broken thing shitting all over the house. It was in no position to fly anywhere. The light in its eyes was rapidly fading as I cupped its shattered body against my chest, the cold biting fiercely at my bare hands, and I knew my father was right. The bird was dying. He didn't have very long left to live, and I was well aware of it. I couldn't just snap its neck, though. I couldn't. When my father grew impatient with me, realizing that I wasn't going to kill the creature in my hands, he tried to snatch it away from me so he could get the job done himself.

I ran.

I ran out of the yard and down the side of our duplex, vaulting over the toppled, dented trash cans, shimmying past mountains of heaped black garbage bags that were spilling their guts out onto the cracked paving stones between the building and the graffitied fence that separated our home from the dingy women's shelter next door.

I hooked a left and ran down the street, past a row of rusting eighties muscle cars and Mr. Wellan's broken down Ford F250. I dodged puddles, not caring when I couldn't dodge them, when my flimsy tennis shoes sank into the shallow pools, immediately soaking wet through. I wasn't dressed for being outside. I'd been eating dinner—fish fingers and dehydrated mashed potato—when the bird had careened into the kitchen window, startling my mother, so I'd been wearing my pajama bottoms and a thin t-shirt. Outside, with the crisp winter air stabbing at all the bare parts of my body, I was aware that it was too cold to be dashing about like

2

a madman in next to nothing, but I didn't have a choice. My father wasn't going to give me one. I'd seen that mean, spiteful look in his eyes before. I knew he wouldn't be happy until the little sparrow or blue jay or whatever it was was dead.

I ran until my feet went numb, either from the cold or from the pounding of the sidewalk underneath them. Eventually, I stopped in the doorway of a breakfast diner, panting, my heart racing, eyes stinging. I couldn't tell if they were stinging because of the cold and the running, or because I didn't want the bird to die and I knew there was no avoiding it. I didn't over analyze. I just held the bird to my chest and tried to catch my breath.

I stood there for a long time, pressing my back against the prickly brick wall of the breakfast diner every time someone wanted to go in or out, pretending not to notice their concerned or annoyed expressions as they went about their business. Slowly, softly, carefully, I stroked the pad of my index finger over the bird's broken wings, over his back, so, so gently over his tiny head. Every time I did that, he closed his eyes, only to open them again, staring up at me, obviously afraid, obviously dying.

After a very long time, he didn't open his eyes again. His minuscule heart stopped fluttering against the palm of my hand, and his wings stopped twitching and shaking. I carried him back home, dragging my feet, feeling like I'd lost a battle somehow. I'd known I couldn't save him, and yet the fact that he'd died in my hands felt like I'd failed him somehow. I should have been able to outrun death. I should have been able to carry him far from it, helped him escape his fate somehow, but it hadn't happened. It hadn't been possible. I'd let him down.

That was a long time ago, now, and yet I still remember the tiny bird and his blue tinged wings. I remember how small he'd felt in my hands. I remember how damaged and hopeless he was, and I remember the sorrowful look in his eyes as he lay cradled against me, his life slipping away. I remember it all too well now, as I hold my sister against me in the back of the ambulance, clinging to her, refusing to let the EMTs take her from me, because she feels the same as that small bird. Like her life is slipping away from her and there's nothing I can do about it.

"Sir. Sir, you really need to put her down now, sir. We can't monitor her properly if you don't." The woman with the paramedic's jacket zipped tightly up underneath her chin holds out her hand to me, imploring me to cooperate with her eyes as well as her words. "We need to take a proper look at her, Mason. She's going to be right here the whole time."

Above us, the siren on top of the ambulance wails urgently, frantic and bullish. White spots dance in my eyes. Millie's legs jerk over and over again as she seizes, her tiny toes curled unnaturally tight against the soles of her feet. The EMT breathes slowly, hand still held out to me, eyes locked on mine, and I see something in her that gives me the strength to let go of my sister and place her down on the gurney next to me. I feel like I've betrayed her in the worst way as the woman, a stranger, begins to check Millie's vitals.

"Pulse is shallow. Pupils dilated. Non responsive." She swings around, pinning me to the wall of the ambulance with her surgical gaze. She seems far too calm as she says, "Has your sister been diagnosed with any pre-existing conditions?"

"Fuck, yes, of course she has!" I slam my hand against the wall beside me, trying to breathe, to stay in control, but it's so fucking hard. "I explained everything to the woman who took the 911 call. She has Lennox Gastaut Syndrome.

The EMT nods through my angry words. "I'm sorry, Mason. They give us as much information as they can, but we have to check. We have to be sure before we can administer any treatment. I promise you, we're going to take care of Millie, but right now you need to give me a rundown of her history, okay? As quick as you can. Is she taking any prescription medication?"

This makes me laugh. Millie's been downing a cock-tail of multi-colored pills twice daily since she was a baby. I reel off the list of Millie's anti-seizure meds that I work my fingers to the bone to pay for, and the EMT nods some more as she checks Millie's airway and pinches her hard on her arm.

I'm used to this. I'm used to people poking and prodding at my tiny, tiny sister, but it never gets any easier. I know she'll be black and blue by the end of this episode. That's best-case scenario. Worst-case scenario: she's hospitalized for days. She gets pneumonia like she did last year, where she had to spend eight days in an induced coma so that her body could heal. She misses school and her friends. I have to leave her there in the children's ward, despite how much it kills me to say goodbye to her every morning, because I have to go to work to pay for her healthcare.

The bills are always more than my paycheck. I always seem to manage to scrape enough cash together to cover her, though. I'm terrified that one day that won't be the case. Maybe one day she'll get sick and I won't have worked enough hours at the garage. I won't have put in any overtime. I won't have curried favor with Mac, and he'll have given his extra work to David or maybe even Marcus.

The EMT rifles in her jump bag, looking for something. She produces a hypodermic needle and a glass bottle filled with clear liquid, and she smiles. "This is clobazam. Should make your little sister feel more like herself soon enough."

It won't, though. Millie reacts badly to clobazam, but there's nothing else that will bump her out of the seizure. She's going to be throwing up for hours when she emerges from this fucked up state; the last time this happened, I had to hold her all night while she cried and fucking puked everywhere. It was better than this, though. It was better than seeing her eyes unfocused and vacant as her whole body shook and threatened to rip itself apart.

I watch as the EMT efficiently administers the contents of the hypodermic into the crook of my little sister's elbow, and I cover my mouth, waiting, hoping that Millie sucks in a deep breath and snaps out of this shit right now.

Come on. Come on. Come on, please...

My heart is tripping over itself, staggering to get me through this moment. My peripherals are a blur. The only thing I see is Millie—her perfectly formed head kicked back, the tendons in her neck straining under her skin like cables pulled taut, her hands, a quarter of the size of my own, twitching, fingers opening and closing involuntarily. *Come on, Millie. Come on, baby girl. You can do this. You got this. Come* on.

Nothing happens.

"I'm going to give her something else, some sodium valproate, Mason. It's okay. It's normal for people to need a little kick sometimes."

She doesn't realize how many times I've been through this. She doesn't realize that I know twenty CCs of anything is abnormal. Well, unless it's being administered to a fully-grown male. It definitely shouldn't be shot into the circulatory system of a miniscule six-year-old human being. I keep my lips clamped tightly shut, though. I watch as the EMT does her job, handling Millie carefully as she gives her what she needs.

This is fucking bullshit.

Such fucking bullshit.

Millie pulls in a ragged, drowning gasp, her eyelids fluttering as she drags herself free of her seizure. She makes a pained, sorrowful keening sound, like an animal caught in a bear trap, and then her eyes roll back into her head and she's unconscious.

"Probably for the best," the EMT says. "Better for her body to take a beat, I reckon. She's okay now. She'll be okay, just you wait and see."

Millie will be far from okay. I know it. The EMT knows it. She's trying to be kind, to be reassuring by feeding me white lies, but her casual blurring of the truth only serves to make me angry. When have lies ever solved a problem? And when has blind ignorance ever helped a person prepare for what is to come?

As the ambulance tears through the streets of Seattle, following a route I have seared into my head like a goddamn brand, I have to remember to breathe. If I don't, I'm going to tear this EMT a new one, I won't be able to stop myself, and that won't help anyone. Least of all Millie.

Sloane

Nothing shocks me anymore. *Nothing*. I've seen it all. Motor vehicle accidents are the worst. The ones where people are brought into the trauma room, talking, asking questions, concerned over their loved ones, maybe complaining of a mild stomach ache but otherwise seemingly okay. And then the next minute their skin is ash and they're coding, and the mild stomach ache they were telling you not to fuss over actually turns out to be severe internal bleeding, their organs mashed to a pulp, and they're dying because it's too late, it's far too late for anything, and then it's all over.

Shock. Shock does strange things to the human body. It numbs you, keeps you running, functioning when you should be still. You don't even realize your injuries are far greater than you first thought until things have progressed past the point of no return, and then that's it. The end. Nothing to be done.

I see this happen. Every. Single. Day.

"What have we got?" I pull gloves on as I stand outside the front of the hospital, waiting for the ambulance to show up. This is my first call this shift; it's been a quiet morning, which is good considering everyone is out sick with the flu and we're operating on a skeleton staff. I didn't have to shoulder anyone out of the way to take this call, and that's a rarity for sure. Normally people are climbing over one another to get to the 'loading dock,' as the interns so eloquently call it, especially when the patient en route might require surgery. All surgical staff must maintain an average of hours in the OR to comply with St. Peter's competencies policy; claiming a patient before anyone else can get to them is often the difference between learning on the job or spending hours at the end of the month trapped in a starkly lit skills lab in your free time, and free time isn't something folk around these parts like to part with unless one hundred percent necessary.

"Little girl," Gitte, one of the nurses tells me. She's new—young but very efficient. The nurses like to haze new members of their team when they arrive, a real trial by fire, and Gitte was no exception. However, unlike most new team members, Gitte handled every situation with grace and ease. When faced with the most intense trauma cases, she remained stoic. She was the epitome of cool, calm and collected. When told she needed to clean bedpans and change catheters for an entire shift, she didn't complain. Instead, she accepted the clipboard Gracie, the head nurse, handed to her and she went and found her first patient, smiling kindly, talking to each person as she moved from room to room.

That was the biggest test. Usually seasoned nurses—any health care provider, really—will think themselves above the basest of tasks after a couple of years treading water in a trauma unit. To come in and accept bed pan duty with a smile and actual interest in each and every patient is, well, it's almost impossible.

"The EMTs have scanned her info ahead. Millie Reeves, six-years-old. History of Lennox Gastaut Syndrome, with both tonic and myoclonic seizures. Previously admitted to St Peter's four times in the past eight months, as well as twice over at Halle and Prentice Medical. She seized for approximately eight minutes in the ambulance. Patient is still unconscious."

I mentally store this information. "Meds?"

"Both clobazam and sodium valproate in the field."

"Jesus. Risky." Administering clobazam and sodium valproate together can be very effective, but you also need to know exactly what you're fucking doing, otherwise you'll end up killing the patient. The EMTs are well trained, though. There's no way they would ever administer a drug if it weren't necessary. "Have pediatrics paged. Let them know they have a regular on the way in. Is Dr. Massey here today?"

Gitte frowns. She scans the tablet she's holding in her hands, presumably searching through the on-call roster to see who's working this morning. She shakes her head. "He's not meant to be here," she says. "I swear I saw him in the ICU an hour ago, though."

She could have done. Oliver Massey's brother was recently brought into the hospital with serious internal injuries; Alex, a fire fighter, had been crushed while trying to help drag an unconscious woman from a car wreck. He's been recovering well from his extensive surgeries, but not well enough to make it out of intensive care. Not yet, anyway.

"See if you can find him. Tell him I'd love a consult if he has the time."

Gitte nods, slips her tablet into the pocket of her scrubs and hurries back into the hospital building. I'm left alone, fingers twitching, heart bouncing around in my chest, adrenalin zipping through me, making my stomach pitch and yaw. It's early but Seattle is already wide-awake and charging. In the midst of the city, St Peter's Hospital is at the heart of things. Located at the convergence of three different neighborhoods, you can't see or hear the docks from here but you can smell them, the sharp bite of salt in the air, and you can *feel* somehow that you're close to the water.

Somewhere on the other side of the city, Zeth Mayfair is thrashing the living shit out of a heavy bag, his hands hopefully wrapped up tight as he works out his early morning frustrations. For a second I lose myself, thinking about how the muscles in his back flex and pop as he hits and swings at that bag. The way he moves is animalistic, raw and dangerous. It would be all too easy to lose a full day watching him work out and train in his fighting gym. All too easy indeed. There are people here that need me, though. People here that need saving.

That thought brings me rushing back into the present. I love Zeth, more than I ever knew was possible, but I figured out a long time ago that I can't allow him to linger in my thoughts here in this place. It's not safe.

I try not to think about the sound of his fists thudding forcefully into the heavy bag. I try not to think about the intoxicating smell of his sweat as he trains. I try not to let myself melt as I remember how hard fighting makes him.

I try not to think at all.

I wait another two minutes before I hear the approaching ambulance. If six-year-old Millie Reeves isn't seizing anymore, there's no real need for the wailing Doppler shift of the sirens, or the frantic flash of the red and blue lights on top of the vehicle that I see speeding into the St Peter's parking lot, but sometimes the EMTs will leave them blaring in order to get their patient to us in good time.

I barely register who's driving the ambo or who's climbing out of the back with the patient. All I care about is the child, and what I can do to fix her. I'm faced with the little girl on the gurney. She's so, so small. Smaller than any six-year-old should be. It would be less surprising if her chart showed she was four years old instead, but no, the paper I'm handed on a clipboard confirms her age as six. I check her vitals, all of which are weak and stressed but within acceptable ranges, and then I take hold of her hand, squeezing it in my own. That's when I look up. That's when I see the tall guy hovering beside the gurney, anxiety vibrating off him in spiky waves.

He doesn't say anything. He looks me dead in the eye and challenges *me* to say something. I get the impression he'll implode if I utter words he doesn't like, however, and that makes me uneasy. I thank the EMTs, noting vaguely that the ambulance was dispatched from Alex Massey's firehouse, and then I turn to the young guy in front of me. "You're Millie's father?" I don't wait for him to respond. I begin pushing the gurney inside. I need to get Millie up to pediatrics and hooked up to an IV as soon as possible.

"No. Brother. I'm her legal guardian, though. Our parents are dead. I've taken care of Millie since she was born, pretty much."

"I see."

"No, you don't."

"I'm sorry?"

"You don't *see*. Unless you've been caring for a seriously ill little girl for the past six years, how can you?" His attitude is really shitty—shitty enough that I stop pushing the gurney and spin on him. I'm not pissed at him. He's too young to be dealing with this responsi-bility. He's barely an adult himself, but he's clearly not thinking straight right now.

"Look around you, Mr. Reeves. Look at where you are. No, I haven't been caring for one sick little girl for the past six years. I've been caring for twenty of them. *Thirty*. I've been caring for seriously ill one-day-olds right along side seriously ill eighty-year-olds. *For a decade.*"

He has the humility to look away. "You're right. I'm sorry. I'm just…"

"Stressed out and scared?"

"Yeah. Exactly."

"It's okay. I know what that feels like, too. Come on. Let's get your sister comfortable and we can talk about where we go from here."

TWO

Zeth

Violence isn't a choice. It's a state of being. It's simply your nature. There's no running from it. No fucking hiding. And even if there was a way to shake the coding of your DNA and hide from your truth, what would be the point? Being violent feels good. Roaring as you smash your fists over and over into some weak piece of shit's torso feels good. Watching the blood spray from people's noses and mouths as your knuckles connect with their faces? Guess what? That feels good, too.

Only a certain few people in this world understand how liberating it feels to pound on someone's head until they lose consciousness. Likewise, it's just as liberating to have your head pounded on. At least you know you're alive. At least you know you're experiencing everything you can, 'cause you can feel it no matter what. And that's what life is, right? Experiencing? Feeling? Bleeding?

My phone's ringing on the other side of the gym, but I can't answer it right now. It's probably Michael, checking in to see if I need him for anything today. I'm midway through handing a Brazilian dude's ass to him, so the call is gonna have to wait.

Blood hits the canvas. Could be mine. Could be his. Who fucking cares? We are both savages, and we're both giving in to our most primal urges to dominate. The only difference between me and the guy I'm matched against right now is that I won't quit. I won't give in. It'll be a chilly day in the underworld before that happens. I don't give a fuck who he is, how big he is, how bad the odds are. I'll *die* before I submit.

The Brazilian guy I've just tossed against the metal links of the cage I've had constructed in the gym spits on the boards and wipes his mouth with the back of his hand. He jerks his head toward my phone, frowning, sweat running down his face.

"Important? You need to get that?" he gasps.

Why can't people go three full rounds without trying to come up with an excuse to call a time out? There's always something: *my wraps are coming loose. My eyes are stinging. I can't remember if I left the oven on at home.* These motherfuckers all know what they're getting into when they step into the cage with me. They've all stood by and laughed as I've knocked people out cold, broken noses and stripped countless guys of their dignity. But no, they're convinced *they're* going to be the one to put *me* down. Has to happen sometime, after all, I hear them whispering to each other. Pretty difficult to hear them whispering later, when they're faces are swollen and bloody like freshly ground meat and their jaws are wired shut. Still, they come back and train. Still, they're on the doorstep every morning, wanting to spar, to receive more punishment, because they're intrigued.

I don't pause to get my phone. My opponent throws up his hands and defends himself at the last second, as if he's hoping I'll change my mind and turn my back on the fight after all. I rain down a succession of jabs on him that probably don't hurt all that much but are hard enough to daze him. He can't know which way is up. When I pause, bringing my own clenched fist back up into a guard position, my opponent straightens, relieved the assault is over from the look on his face, only to drop like a sack of shit to the floor when I power my right knee up and drive it into his side.

Suck on that, asshole.

He makes a gasping, sucking noise, wheezing help-lessly on the ground as I stalk around him, considering my options. He probably has at least two broken ribs right now. Do I give him chance to tap out on the fight, or should I be merciless? I could get down and grapple with him, easily getting him in a chokehold while he's vulnerable. It would be lights out for Mr. Brazil in less than eight seconds if he doesn't do something beside flop around like a fish out of water.

My phone is still ringing.

If I don't choke him out, I could always get him in an arm bar. Break that shit, too. I pace around him like a lion, looking for other possibilities.

My phone begs for attention.

I could get him in mount. Lean on his chest. Make him gasp some more. I could straddle the fucker and have done with him once and for all. Nothing like some ground and pound to finish a fight quickly. The guy rolls onto his good side, curling his knees into his chest, his eyes rolling, the whites visible. He must be in a shitload of pain.

My phone grows louder somehow.

"Fuck's sake." It's impossible to fucking concentrate like this. Mr. Brazil is going to have to wait a moment. I plan on grabbing my phone and silencing the damn thing, but when I drop down out of the cage, the soles of my sneakers scuffing on the dusty concrete floor, and I make it over to my cell, I see a number on the screen that won't bear ignoring. Or rather, I'd be smart not to ignore in the least.

It's a New Mexico number.

I shoot a glance back toward the cage where my opponent is now on his knees, right arm braced across his stomach, head hanging low as he tries to figure out his shit. I doubt he's going anywhere any time soon. I'll head back to help him in a second—Sloane will crucify me if I hurt a gym member and then didn't give them medical attention afterward—but I'm undoubtedly about to have a conversation that shouldn't be conducted out in the open.

I head up to my office, running up the stairs, taking them three at a time, and I slam the door closed behind me. "Yeah?"

"Hey, brother-in-law. What's new?" Once upon a time, I would have been a weapons-grade asshole to the man on the other end of the line, but these days Louis James Aubertin the third and I have a more congenial arrangement. He's married to my girlfriend's sister after all. And apparently this is what family is all about: playing nice.

"Didn't think I'd hear from you any time soon," I tell him. "How's life in the dust bowl?"

"Dusty," Rebel agrees. "Hot." He pauses, and then says, "*Busy.*"

His 'busy' is most people's 'dangerous.' I'd like to argue that it would be closer to my own 'status quo' but hey. Who's got time for a dick-measuring contest when they have injured foreigners trying to catch their breath twenty feet away? "Sounds ominous. Care to elaborate?" I ask.

Rebel laughs softly. "A mutual friend of ours has left town. I had one of my guys check up on her whereabouts. Seems like she's headed your way."

I know perfectly well who this mutual friend is. For the past year or so, ever since I got involved with Sloane

20

and her reckless mission to find her missing sister come hell or high water, DEA Agent Denise Lowell has been sticking her nose into our business, generally making a nuisance of herself and pissing me off in the process. It can only be her.

"Why the change in location? Any idea?"

"None, I'm afraid. Her files have been sealed. Even our hacker can't break into that shit without setting off a few alarm bells."

Frustrating, but not the end of the world. I have hackers of my own who don't give a shit about alarm bells. "Appreciate the heads up."

"No problem. Figured you might like warning before she showed up on your doorstep."

I pull at my hand wraps, tightening them as I lean against the wall of the office. "I doubt she's here for me. I'm not involved in drugs."

Rebel makes a bemused sound, the line crackling loudly as he laughs. "Dude. If I remember correctly, you stole the woman's dog. And you professionally embarrassed her. *Repeatedly*. Doesn't matter if you have five keys of coke jammed up your asshole or you're a poster boy for Narcotics Anonymous. You can bet good money on her coming for you if she gets the opportunity."

I grunt, scratching at my jaw. "True. That bitch needs to develop a new hobby. This shit is getting really old, really fast."

"Couldn't agree more, man. Still…forewarned is forearmed, right?"

I smile a grim smile. "Oh, I'll be armed alright."

I say no more. I don't tell him about the fact that I've known Lowell is in town for a while now. I don't tell him that I've been going against everything I stand for, keeping it from Sloane. I don't tell him I've been keeping my eye on Mason, the kid I've been training with every morning, ever since I saw him talking to the DEA agent outside Macs a few weeks ago, either. I keep my mouth shut, and Rebel hangs up the phone.

••••

I bundle Mr. Brazil up and send him on his merry way—he insisted he didn't want to go to the hospital, so what the fuck could I do but let him go?—and then I wait for Michael to show up. The gym is empty. Mason, the spy in our midst, was supposed to be here training first thing this morning before he started work across the road at the auto mechanics' place, but he never showed, so I have the whole place to myself. The fees at Blood & Roses fighting gym are astronomically high, so only the most serious people come and train here. Means the place isn't overrun with teenagers whose balls have just dropped and don't have a fucking clue what they're doing. Also means Seattle's criminal element tends to stay away, which is exactly what I was hoping for. Whenever a guy wants to apply for membership, I have

Michael perform a very in-depth background search on them, making sure they're not going to bring trouble to our doorstep. The faintest whiff of underground bullshit, and their applications are rejected with no explanation as to why.

Michael arrives at the gym around midday and drops his workout bag on the ground by the roller doors, sagging against the metal frame. He looks like shit. I tell him this, which doesn't seem to help in any way but entertains me greatly.

"Screw you, man. I haven't slept in thirty-six hours," he informs me, pressing the tips of his fingers into his eye sockets. "I'm getting old. I can't do this shit anymore."

"Why the fuck haven't you slept? Better not be moonlighting for someone else," I growl.

"Of course not. I'm just...it's personal."

"*Personal*?" I want to smirk, but I manage to rein in the urge. Personal means fucking. No, scratch that. Personal means *hard-core* fucking. Michael's always been a bit of a closed book when it comes to his life outside of my employ, and that's never bothered me. Too many guys don't shut up about where they're sticking their dicks, and I'd rather Michael kept his cards close to his chest over him incessantly talking about the chicks he's seeing. I'll admit to being faintly curious right now, though. Only faintly.

Michael rolls his eyes. "It's not what you're thinking,"

he informs me.

"I'm thinking you've been awake for thirty-six hours because you've been entertaining someone."

"Okay, so you're not completely wrong. But it's...it's more complicated than that."

It always is. Especially where women are concerned. I don't push him to spill any further information. If he wants to share, he will. In the meantime, we have a DEA agent to track down. Michael's up to speed on the Lowell fiasco already. Well, he knows as much as I do—that the woman's back in town and looking to make trouble. He seems unsurprised when I fill him in on the fact that Rebel called and confirmed this, though. He keeps quiet as we close up the gym and climb into the Camaro. He's extra fucking quiet as we head across town toward the warehouse, where I used to spend at least seventy percent of my time before I met Sloane and ended up moving into her secluded spot on the hill. Not a word passes between us in over thirty minutes. Michael sits motionless in the seat next to me, carved out of rock as I gun the Camaro's engine, sliding a little too quickly through the corners. He finally protests when I run a stop sign three blocks from the docklands.

"What the hell, man? You drive the most ostentatious, over the top car ever sold. You're speeding, and now you're running stop signs? If a cop pulls you over, they're gonna think they've won the motherfucking lottery. You want to spend the rest of the day locked up while five-oh figures out what they can pin on you besides reckless driving?"

I shrug, taking another hair-raising right hand turn. "Just thought you might like waking up," I tell him.

Michael growls. "I'm perfectly awake, boss."

This is flame retardant bullshit and he knows it. I let him off, though, because he's earned it. "Just tell me one thing. Is this bizarre, edgy Michael because the bitch is back in our lives? Or is there something else I should know about?" I don't have a clue what could possibly be more inconvenient than Denise Lowell entering the Seattle city limits, but shit. Things have been quiet. *Too* quiet. It'd be grand to believe that this is just how life will be now—predictable and safe, because that's what Sloane deserves. But I'm not that stupid. It's my experience that life will pitch you a curve ball or five when you're least expecting it, and they're always the ones that fuck you up the most. And when it rains, it motherfucking pours.

Michael presses his fingertips against his mouth, elbow propped up against the window of the Camaro. He stares up at the warehouse as we pull up outside, a grimace twisting his features. "I don't know," he says quietly. "I just...I have a bad feeling is all."

THREE

Sloane

Millie Reeves doesn't cry when she wakes up. She vomits and complains that she's cold, but that's it. All things considered, she's relatively lucky. She was breathing when she was having the violent seizure that brought her here to St Peter's, but the oxygen supply to her brain could easily have been compromised. She could have woken up with altered brain function or damage to numerous aspects of her nervous system, and yet she seems as though she's coping admirably. Unfortunately the same can't be said for her brother.

"I don't care what the doctor said. I want to take her home!" Mason Reeves is hot headed and reactive right now, as he leans across the reception desk, growing redder and redder as he tries to brow beat Gracie. Little does he know that his efforts are completely pointless.

I see Gracie raise her do-not-fuck-with-me-family-member-of-a-patient shield. "And *I* don't care what you want, Mr. Reeves. Your sister is in recovery. That means she is *re-cov-er-ing.* Do you understand what I'm saying?"

"I understand that she can recover at home, ma'am. Now, please. Let me sign the paperwork so I can get her out of here."

"I'm afraid I can't do that, *sir*. Now please step away from this desk before I call security." Gracie's jaw is fixed and locked, raised. She's just waiting for him to argue some more. Of course, what she's doing is highly illegal. Mason is Millie's legal guardian. She doesn't specifically require urgent care, so he's well within his rights to take her whenever he wants. Gracie's just one of those women who will push and push in order to get her own way, and to hell with the consequences.

I quicken my pace as I head toward them, grinding my teeth. "Is everything okay here, Mason? Are you looking for an update on Millie?"

He barely casts his eyes in my direction as he acknowledges what I've said. "Millie Reeves. Six-years-old. Diagnosed with LSG at aged three years, three months. Suffered a major grand mal seizure in the last twelve hours. Now showing positive signs of improvement, despite continuous vomiting and diarrhoea. Blood pressure is normal. All cognitive signs reported normal. Will require constant monitoring for the next forty-eight hours to ensure no long term damage has occurred as a result of potential oxygen deprivation." Mason stops there. He swivels his head so he's looking right at me now. "Is there anything else, Dr. Romera, or have I got everything?"

Damn. He's on the verge of snapping. I've seen it on so many people. There's a flicker people get in their eyes, a visible fracture in their temper that could either splinter them open or shut them down at a moment's notice. "You obviously have a very good understanding of your sister's condition, Mason. I'm impressed at the level of care you've been giving her. Let me ask you, though...do you think you can give her the same level of care at home that we can give her here at the hospital?"

He clenches his jaw. "I'm not fucking stupid, okay? I know I'm fucking up. I know she deserves better than I can give to her, but I'm trying. I'm doing my best. Of course she'd be better off here, but I can't afford to keep her here longer than she absolutely has to be. This wasn't her worst seizure. There are plenty more to come, and I need to make sure I can afford *those* five-star visits to the wonderful St. Peter's of Mercy hospital."

Gracie shoots me a complicated look. It contains many mixed emotions: worry; anxiety; stoicism; and lastly, guilt. The last flash of remorse is undoubtedly because of what she did a few months ago. She told the DEA she'd seen me sneaking out of the hospital, carrying bags of blood I needed to save Zeth's life. Lowell tried to threaten me with the fact that I'd been caught stealing from St. Peter's. I nearly lost my job. I nearly lost *everything*. To say things have been awkward between us since I came back to work is an understatement. I don't blame her, though. Denise Lowell is a conniving cunt who will always get her way. Gracie has a kid to take care of. Her own job to think about. I'm sure Lowell implied she'd lose both if she didn't tell her everything about me when she came calling at the hospital.

"So can I take her? Or shall I call the police?" Mason folds his arms across his chest, huffing heavily down his nose.

Exasperated, I scramble to think of a way to keep him here. He hasn't been unreasonable. He hasn't said anything that isn't true. The seizure Millie just had was bad, yes, but given the nature of her condition it really won't be her worst. The worst is yet to come. LSG might not kill her, but in the same vein it could. Mason's essentially saving for his sister's funeral. I wonder if he realizes that. I squeeze the pen I'm clenching in my hand, digging my fingernail into the hard plastic. "Look. Just give me an hour, Mason. Give me one last chance to look her over. If she really is stable enough, I'll let you take her."

His eyes flash. "And if she's not stable enough?"

"Then...then I don't know. We'll cross that bridge when we come to it." It's a pretty poor answer to his question, but it's all I've got at the moment. I'm a doctor, though. A problem solver. Give me a pair of stockings and a rubber band and I'll figure out how to stop someone bleeding out. Give me an hour and a cell phone, and I'll figure out how to make sure Millie Reeves receives the care she needs and deserves. Mason doesn't believe in me yet, but he will. He blinks, the muscles in his jaw working overtime.

"I'm—I'm supposed to be at work," he says. "I don't have an hour."

"Then give me *eight*. Go to work. Come back later on this evening and I'll have this figured out, I swear I will."

Mason doesn't say anything. He shifts from one foot to the other, his right shoulder lifting up and down as he looks from me to Gracie and back again. "She'll look after her," Gracie says softly. "She's an excellent doctor. We'll call the second anything changes with your sister, Mr. Reeves." She already has her hand on his arm, ushering him out of the reception; she doesn't give him the option of refusing the suggestion. The anger and the frustration that was spilling out of him a second ago seems to have fizzled out in the past few seconds. I've seen it happen many times before; the weight of responsibility is a heavy, heavy thing. Making difficult decisions on a daily basis is crippling. Carrying around the burden of someone else's care every single hour of every single day is enough to bow someone's back to the point of breaking. The second someone offers to relieve you of that burden, people are often too shocked to react.

I watch Gracie walk Mason out of the building, and I feel the weight of my assumed burden pressing in already. God knows how the poor guy has borne it for so long.

••••

I find Oliver Massey furiously washing his hands in the residents' lounge. He cuts me a sideways glance when he notices me slipping through the door. "Goddamn flu bug. There are barely any nurses in the ICU. How the hell are you supposed to operate an intensive care unit when there is no staff to intensively care for anyone? *Jesus.*" He takes a step back when water sloshes over the side of the deep stainless steel trough he's bending over. His suit pants slowly turn from grey to black at the hem where the water has drenched them. "Great." Oliver picks up a towel from the neat stack beside him and pats himself down, grumbling under his breath.

"You okay? Is *Alex* okay?" Oliver's usually pretty up-beat, no matter how shitty his day has been. His current bad mood is likely related to his brother's condition.

Oliver throws the towel into the laundry bin by the lockers and sighs heavily; his chin rests on his chest as he leans, resting his back against the row of steel locker doors. "Who the fuck knows," he says quietly. "He should be on a recovery ward by now, Sloane. He should be back at fucking work or something, not still hooked up to life support."

Anything I might say seems futile. Oliver knows the lines we feed to people when their loved ones are fighting for recovery, because he feeds them to people too: it's a process. These things take time. The only thing we can do now is wait. We avoid giving false hope. We skirt around words like hope altogether, because it gives the impression that the situation is no longer within our control. Hope implies an unknowable force has taken the reins on their brother/mother/sister/daughter's health, and we are nothing more than mere bystanders, peering through a window, lips bitten between our teeth and fingers crossed behind our backs.

Instead of trying to placate him, I ask him this instead: "What can I do?"

Oliver's shoulders slump. He's a picture of exhaustion. "I don't know. Something? Nothing?" He spins around and props himself up against the locker beside me, and I suspect he'd crumple to the ground without the rigid metal's support. "*Anything*?" he says, breathing out loud and slow. "We're trained for this. We're trained to detach ourselves, and I thought fuck yeah. I have this. I can do this. If anyone I love is ever rushed through those trauma doors, I'll be able to switch it off. There won't be time to have a meltdown. I know I'll be able to do everything in my power to fix them, and my hands won't be shaking as I do it. I'll be determined. Focused. Because that's what they drill into us, how they teach us to be."

"And you were, Oliver. You *were* all of those things. You didn't flinch once when they brought Alex in. You were single minded and you got the job done. *You saved his life.*"

My words wash over Oliver like water over rock. He doesn't feel them, doesn't allow them to affect him in any way. "Maybe," he whispers, staring down at his hands. He gives me a thin, hangdog smile, kind of watery around the edges. "Maybe you're right. Maybe I did do everything right in that operating room. But fuck, Sloane. They don't equip us to deal with this part. We're never taught to feel like them, the people pacing the hallways like caged lions because they feel...because they feel so fucking *useless.*"

They really don't teach us that. It's not in a doctor's nature to sit back and let time do its job, as we advise so many other people to do every day. We're relentless in nature—or at least good doctors should be. There's no giving up. No patience. Our lives—especially the lives of trauma surgeons—are lived in five-second bursts. So much can change in those fleeting five seconds. Lives are made and broken. Loved ones survive, and loved ones are lost. Oliver and I were trained that every single second passing by is a grain of sand trickling through our fingers, one we will never be able to snatch back, and it is our duty to make each and every one of them count. So waiting for a trauma surgeon? Waiting is an impossibility. A torturous concept that would cripple even the most pragmatic of us. Oliver must be going out of his mind.

"I need your help with something," I tell him. This is the kindest thing I can possibly do—give him some other purpose to take his mind off his brother. "I have a situation, a tricky one, and I need your huge brain to come up with a solution for me."

Oliver's eyes flicker to the ceiling, and they stay there. "I'm not on shift, Sloane."

"I'm aware."

"Then I can't just go interfering in your cases." This is hospital policy—If a doctor isn't on duty, he or she may not work on patients in any way, shape or form. They could have been drinking. They could have been doing any manner of questionable things before they walked through the entranceway of St. Peter's of Mercy Hospital. They're not mentally prepped to take on whatever they might be faced with, so they're not permitted to even touch a patient. Oliver may be breaking that rule with Alex today, but he can get away with that. The chief's given up trying to keep him away from his brother, but it will be another matter entirely if she catches him consulting on a different patient.

"You don't need to interfere at all. You don't even need to see the kid," I say. "I just need some help figuring out how to keep her here."

"The kid?"

"A little girl, suffers from severe grand mal seizures. Her older brother's her legal guardian, and he can't afford to keep her in for another few days."

"Is she likely to seize again?"

Now it's my turn to shrug. "I don't know. There's a risk. She's stable for the most part."

"Then send her home, Sloane. Let the guy minimize the costs."

I'm surprised by this response. Oliver's usually a proponent for as much observation as the situation can afford. "She'd be better off admitted for the next two days at least," I point out.

An anguished look flashes across Oliver's face. "Can we prevent her from seizing again?"

"No."

"Can we re-admit her later if her brother's insurance won't cover her?"

I don't even need to answer this one.

"Then you know what you need to do," Oliver says flatly. "Send her home with her brother. Let her recuperate in her own bed, and give her brother some peace of fucking mind."

FOUR

Zeth

We draw yet another blank at the warehouse. The calls we've been making for days now have all ended the same: no one knows what Lowell is up to. No one knows what her purpose is here, and no one wants to get involved, either.

Michael and I spend six hours kicking over rocks, seeing what we can discover, but the time is wasted. The bitch could be back on vacation for all we know, come to check out Pike Place Markets and the E.M.P, and we'd be none the wiser.

There is one person we could ask, of course. Mason obviously knows what she wants. He's been asking weird, probing questions about my life, trying to tease information out of me, but I can't quite figure out what he's trying to make me spill. I don't want to pin the guy to a wall and demand he tells me what the fuck is going on yet, though. Something's telling me to watch, to wait, to see what happens. Either way, the kid's going to fucking pay. My blood was boiling in my veins for days after I saw him talking to that unmistakable blonde bitch outside Mac's, and it's still simmering quietly now. It won't quiet until I've made the kid hurt for betraying us. Fair enough, he doesn't know me. He doesn't owe me much, aside from the fact that I didn't kick his ass and straight up leave him in the gutter when he first broke into the gym. But there's honor amongst thieves in this shady, dark world we're treading water in, and you can't just go around working with the fucking DEA and expect no one to find out.

Michael and I sit in silence as we drive back into the city, each of us thinking deeply as we slip through the early dusk, heading toward the gym. As we grow closer to our destination, I feel fucking itchy and uncomfortable in my own skin.

Lowell isn't just here for a vacation.

She's here to mess up my shit, just like Rebel said she was. I *did* professionally embarrass her. I *did* steal her dog. Technically, she *gave* Ernie to me at the end, but I doubt she sees it that way. Of course she fucking doesn't. Just when things were starting to look calm, like life was slowing down a little, like I was done dealing with shitty people, done with looking over my shoulder every time I walk out of the house, Lowell shows up again and throws me back in at the deep end. Sure, I could ignore this and let her do her thing, but it won't work out that way. I know it won't. Her arrival in my city is a precursor to terrible, awful things, and I need to be ready for every last one of them. If I'm not, I'm either going to end up dead or back in Chino and neither of those options are acceptable to me. Not now that I have Sloane to think about.

Speaking of which…

My phone, sitting on the dash of the Camaro, chimes, and I see 'Doc' quickly flash up on the screen.

Sloane: Are you busy? I need you, baby.

I immediately throw the car into fifth. "You okay to lock up after you work out?" I ask Michael.

"Sure."

"Great." I burn my way through the last five minutes of the journey, hands clenched tightly around the steering wheel. I'm not worried. If Sloane were in any kind of trouble, she wouldn't have text me to ask if I was busy. She would have called until I picked up. If she absolutely had no other choice but to send a text, she'd have written SOS and nothing else—she knows the procedure if she's threatened in any way.

Still, she needs me. She said she fucking *needs* me, and I won't ever keep her waiting when she sends me a message like that. I drop Michael off, barely stopping for the guy to climb out of the vehicle before I'm tearing off in the direction of the hospital. I find Sloane in St. Peter's deserted loading dock at the rear of the building—she's taken to escaping there when she needs a moment to breathe—sitting on a concrete step where nurses and hospital porters sometimes come to smoke, hiding from their patients and their families.

It's almost dark now, but I can see the pale shape of Sloane's white coat shifting ever so slightly as I jog across the loading dock toward her. She looks up at me as I reach her, unsurprised by my sudden appearance.

"That didn't take you long," she whispers.

"I knew a shortcut."

She scowls, because she knows my shortcuts involve running red lights and undercutting any driver I consider too slow, which is basically everyone else on the road. "My reckless boy. You're gonna end up on a gurney, flat on your back, being wheeled into here one of these days."

I shake my head. "I won't. And if I did, I know a really good doctor. She'd probably put me back together again."

"I don't know about that." She smiles softly. "All the doctors at St. Peter's are out sick. This miracle worker of yours might be feeling a little under the weather, too."

I sit down beside her, wrapping a protective arm around her shoulders. "I thought you'd shaken that cold?" She does look a little grey, actually. Tired, perhaps. I'm not completely stupid, so I don't tell her this, but concern squeezes at my chest. Emotions like this still surprise me. I'm not used to caring about anyone else, especially this deeply. I thought there was a limit to how much one person could care about another, but it turns out I was wrong. It turns out the depths you can love someone are boundless. I don't think I'll ever reach a point where I can truly say I've reached my capacity for caring for this woman. It makes me weak. Vulnerable. It feels dangerous most of the time, but there's nothing I can do about it. I'm fucking addicted to her, and I wouldn't change that for the world.

"So? You *needed* me?" I nuzzle my face into her hair, breathing in deeply. Nothing smells as good as she does. She's been working twelve hours straight and a faint chemical smell clings to her, but it can't mask the scent of her skin and her hair. I close my eyes and I can feel my dick getting hard in my pants.

Sloane knows me inside out. She knows by my inflection on the word need that my mind is already in the gutter, along with the rest of my body, where I'm coincidentally fucking her like an animal. She places one hand on my thigh, her fingertips running up and down the inside seam of my jeans.

"I'm sorry. I probably shouldn't have text you. I'm just having a tough day."

"Violent patient?" My mind instantly goes to these places. If any of those fuckers have been causing trouble for her, they'll leave St Peter's more injured and broken than they went in, I don't give a shit who they are.

Sloane laughs. "No. Just red tape. It's so goddamn frustrating. This little girl needs treatment and her brother's doing his best to provide it for her, but his insurance doesn't even come close to covering her bills. He wants to take her home. I promised him I'd have figured out a way to keep her here by the time he finished work. I have less than two hours to pull a miracle out of thin air."

I watch her as she speaks. Lines of concern have formed between her eyebrows; her cheeks are blushed and red from her annoyance. She's such a strong, fierce, independent person. It's unsurprising that she's so wound up about something so inconsequential as health insurance, or the lack thereof, and the fact that it's preventing her from doing her job.

I plant a kiss on the side of her head, humming deeply. She pulls these reactions from me, and yet she has no fucking idea how badly she affects me. I love how committed she is to her job and to helping others. A lot of people become doctors because of the money, or because of the challenge, and invariably those are the people who end up being bad doctors. The greats, the ones people remember forever, are the ones likely working double shifts just to make sure there are doctors available to help. Just like Sloane is right now. I'd had so little experience with people who genuinely cared about the wellbeing of others that I thought it was all an act when I first met Sloane. It made me uncomfortable. Now, looking at her as she tries to overcome this bureaucratic hurdle so she can take care of a little girl, my heart aches in the strangest of ways. I could never tell her. I could never tell anyone.

Still. It aches.

I brush my hand slowly over her hair, tucking it back. I casually flick out my tongue, stroking the shell of her ear with it as I exhale. Sloane shivers against me, her own breath catching in her throat. "St. Peter's is a big place, isn't it? Surely there's a secluded spot you could hide a bed?" I whisper.

"What do you mean? Hide the kid out of sight and treat her off the books?"

"Mmm. If she really needs the treatment, seems like the best option to me."

"It's not that simple, Zeth. The legal implications are..." She trails off as I probe her ear a little deeper with the tip of my tongue. "The legal implications are dire. I could get into so much trouble. I could...I could lose my job. Worse than that, I could be arrested. I'd have to steal from the hospital again. I—" She can't continue any further, because I've started kissing and biting at her throat. We both already know this option, hiding the little girl, is a foregone conclusion. One she had already made before she even texted me. She just wanted to hear me say it.

I am the devil standing on her shoulder, after all. I am her dark prince, leading her down paths she would never walk alone. Once upon a time, there may have been an angel standing on the other shoulder, but that guy is long gone now. And it wasn't me who scared him away. Sloane chased him off all by herself. She *liked* the darkness. She *liked* the shadows and the adrenalin. Now breaking the rules and chasing down another thrill is all that's left for her.

"Stop, Zeth. God, please...I have to go back inside in a minute. If you carry on doing that—"

"You'll want me to fuck you?" I growl into the delicate curve of her neck. "You'll want me to push your legs open and guide my fingers into your cunt. Don't you want me to see how wet you are, Sloane? Don't you want my fingers slick with you?"

"*Fuck.*"

"You said you had two hours until this guy shows up. It's not going to take that long to move the kid into the basement."

"I have other patients, Zeth. The hospital's barely running as it is. I can't—"

I smirk.

"What are you smiling about, you evil bastard?" She jabs me in the ribs, pretending to be mad.

"Well..." I rub my hand on her leg, my smile growing. "You say one thing with your mouth, angry girl, but your body is speaking an entirely different language."

43

She looks down at herself and notices what I noticed just a second ago—that her legs are already spread wide open, the tight, professional black pencil skirt she wore to work instead of her scrubs riding up her bare thighs.

"Damn it," she hisses.

"Mmm." I trail my fingers lightly over her smooth skin, my blood surging around my body faster and faster. It's shocking that I can even feel it moving through my veins at all; seems to me the majority of my blood is circulating primarily around my rock solid cock and nowhere else. "You've been working non-stop for days. You haven't slept properly since you got sick. You should be kinder to yourself," I say, grinning from ear to ear. "Or at least let me be kind to you. To your pussy specifically."

She gives me a doubtful look. She wants me just as much as I want her, which is a fucking lot. I can tell by the way her full lips are even more swollen than usual. Her cheeks were already flushed when I sat down next to her, but now they look like they're on fire, hot to touch. Her shoulders are rolled back, arching her spine, pushing out her breasts so that they're straining at her pale blue cotton shirt. The swell of her tits is just visible, heaving against the material, and I have a mind to take hold of her clothing and rent it apart so they can spring free. It's a fucking crime that they're covered so efficiently right now. I want them bare and naked. I want her nipples peaked and hard against the fresh night air. I

44

want her fingers in my hair, tugging on it hard as I massage her flesh there with my tongue.

My dick is throbbing, painful and demanding as Sloane tilts her head down to look at her bare, spread legs. "I suppose..." she whispers.

It's all I need. I'm down on my knees before she can utter another word. I shove my way between her legs, ducking down so that she can put them over my shoulders.

"God, Zeth. I think...I think there are cameras out here."

From my vantage point on my knees, about two seconds away from burying my face in the already wet material of her panties, I send her the faintest of smiles. "Now, now, angry girl. Don't play games with me. You know it turns you on to think of someone on the other end of that camera, watching you come for me."

She shudders, her legs pressing a little tighter around my head. Her lips are parted, the faint gleam of her teeth visible in the half-light. "Maybe you're right," she says quietly. "Maybe I do. Maybe...maybe you should give them something to see."

She's a wicked, wicked girl, and I made her that way. The thought gives me a grim satisfaction. I push her legs open further, sinking lower in between them. She should know better than to tell me I need to put on a show. Putting on a show is one of my favorite things in the whole world. I hook my finger underneath the fabric of her panties, pulling it to one side so that she's exposed to me. "Lay back," I tell her.

Sloane licks her lips, easing herself back onto her elbows, her pristine white lab coat draping onto the concrete. It's going to be filthy by the time I'm finished with her. But then, so will she. "Put your feet here," I tell her, taking hold of her by the ankles and placing the soles of her pumps onto the tops of my thighs.

With the patience of a saint, I allow myself to slowly lean into her. She's trembling like crazy, making small, quiet, urgent sounds. Knowing that I have this much power over her is precious to me. Some people might say that thinking this way is toxic. That *I'm* toxic. But so fucking what? I've never given a single shit over what anyone else thinks of me, and I'm sure as fuck not going to start now.

I love that she obeys me.

I love that she gives herself over to me with perfect, unquestioning abandon.

I love that she trusts me.

I love that she loves me.

I know how hard it is for her to let go and hand me the reins, which is why I cherish moments like these. It's more than sex. It's more than lust. It's everything.

My tongue finally finds its mark, and Sloane's body jumps on the concrete loading dock like she just got electrocuted. "Oh, shit, Zeth. Oh my god." Her hands run up her own body, until she's cupping her breasts through her shirt. There's nothing more enjoyable than watching a woman who knows how to press her own buttons. As I work my mouth over her pussy, growling with pleasure at the taste of her, and the texture of her on my tongue, I watch her touching herself, stroking her fingers against the skin of my neck, over her lips, sliding up under her button-down shirt so she can reach the swell of her perfect tits under her bra as well.

If giving head was a martial art, I'd be a black belt. No, scratch that, I'd be a motherfucking grandmaster. I know exactly how to work the tip of my tongue over Sloane's clit to make her body lock up tight. I know precisely how to use the flat of my tongue, sliding up over her pussy to massage the sensitive bundle of nerves in a long, broad stroke, in order to make her pant and moan.

"Damn it, Zeth. Oh, shit, you're going to make me come!"

Like I said: *Motherfucking Grandmaster.*

I curl my arms up underneath her thighs, so I can grip her better by the hips, and that's when I push my tongue inside her. She tastes so fucking good. I could be stranded on a desert island, and Sloane's pussy could be the only thing available for me to eat, and I'd be the happiest, most well fed man in the existence of human kind. She grabs hold of me by the hair, grinding up into my face, and I almost lose my shit.

She's close. I can tell by how wet she is and the frantic, erratic note in her voice when she moans. I want to make her come with my mouth—it obliterates her every time when I do—but a large part of me, an eight inch long, rock solid, demanding as fuck part of me, wants very much to be inside her right now.

She whimpers as I rock back, leaving her laying there on her back with her legs wide open. "Patience, angry girl."

It takes me less than a second to unzip my pants and free my cock. Sloane watches me through half closed eyes; the first two buttons of her shirt are undone, and her tits are free, the cups of her bra pulled down to expose her creamy, smooth skin, and her peaked nipples. "Bad, bad girl," I tell her. "Look what you've done."

She closes her eyes, head rocking back, and I give myself half a heartbeat to take in the sight before me. Has a man ever been as lucky as this before? The woman in front of me is laid wide open, soul bared, waiting for me to do whatever the fuck I want to her, and it's the most beautiful thing I've ever seen.

I take her. I'm not gentle as I slide myself into her slick, wet heat. I thrust as hard as I can, because I know how much she fucking loves it when I do. She winds her arms around me, pulling me to her, digging her fingernails into my leather jacket. I can feel them through the thick, tough material, so she clearly means business.

God, her pussy feels so good. I've fucked her mouth

and I've fucked her ass, but nothing is ever as good as her pussy. Our bodies fit together with a kind of precision that blows my mind. Our physiology doesn't lie; we were made for each other.

I hit her g-spot, and Sloane lets out a raw, broken cry that pierces me like a goddamn spear to the chest. She's so close. I am, too. The rising feeling of euphoria inside me is something I can pull away from if she ever needs more time, but right now she's teetering on the brink and I'm going to have to quit slamming myself into her if I want her to hold out any longer.

I've teased her enough, though. I want to feel her coming all over my cock right now. I have to feel it, like I have to breathe air. It's more than a desire; it's a necessity. I bite down on her collarbone as I ride the wave that comes rushing at me. Sloane bucks upward, her hips pressing urgently against mine, and then she's screaming out into the dark, her hands clawing at me as she comes.

Heat blooms inside me, spreading its fingers over me, through me, over the backs of my thighs and my buttocks, chasing up my back, sending a riot of pins and needles prickling up the back of my neck, over my scalp. Sloane shakes, her breath coming in short, sharp blasts as I push into her one last time.

"God," she whispers, her voice hoarse, barely audible above the racket my crazy heartbeat is making in my ears right now. "That was...*intense*."

49

She opens her eyes, looking up at me, and I see myself reflected there. I see an endless, improbable, imperfect future stretching out before me. If it *were* perfect, this life Sloane and I have signed up for together, then neither one of us would survive it. We both need a little chaos to fuel our fires. We both need a little unpredictability and a little turbulence along the way. Just knowing that we can handle whatever is thrown at us is enough for me, though.

"I need you to do something for me, Sloane."

She looks half drunk from the fucking I just gave her when she blinks up at me. "What?"

"Don't you dare fucking clean yourself up when you go back inside."

Her eyes widen. "I have dirt all over my clothes, Zeth. I can't go back onto the ward looking like this."

"Get changed by all means. Brush your hair if you have to," I tell her, pinching her ass lightly between my index finger and my thumb. "But don't you dare clean away my come, angry girl. I want you to go back to work, knowing that I'm still inside you. I want you to be able to feel me between your legs. Promise me right fucking now."

She nods slowly, letting out an unsteady breath that makes my balls ache. "I promise," she says.

"Good. Now get back inside, before I decide I want to fuck you all over again."

50

FIVE

Sloane

I'm a train wreck. Thank god nobody sees me as I hurry through the corridors and dash into the change rooms to grab some scrubs and a fresh lab coat. Fuck, that man loves making life difficult for me sometimes. Or if not difficult per se, then interesting in the least. No doubt he's smirking that wicked smirk of his as he drives home, congratulating himself on how my heart is likely thrumming in my chest as I strip out of my filthy clothes, my body now sore and aching, tired from the wild sex we just had. And he's right, it *is* thrumming in my chest, and my body *is* sore and aching, and I feel amazing, lit up from the inside out. How the hell am I supposed to get my head back in the game after that? It's not going to be easy. I intend on keeping the promise I just made to him, so I'm going to be thinking about the wild sex we just had every time I move, sit down or plain breathe. I have to make sure I'm focused at the same time, though. I have a small child to wheel into a basement.

No one says a word as I make my way into Millie Reeves' room and collect her chart from the end of her bed. Her stats are the same as they were earlier today—her BP is low and her heart rate seems a little erratic at times, but other than that she's stable. There's every chance I'm being ridiculous here and the girl would be perfectly fine at home in the care of her brother, but I don't know. For some reason, there's a heavy weight in my stomach, sinking through me like a stone, and the thought of releasing Millie from our care makes me anxious. Her brother clearly looks after her very well, but this nagging, bothersome sensation won't quit. I learned a long time ago that ignoring your gut usually has severe consequences in my line of work. They teach you how to be logical, to work through plausible possibilities and to train yourself to have a scientific brain, as opposed to a brain ruled by emotion, but sometimes you *need* a little emotion.

I've been so distracted by Millie's chart that I've forgotten to check on the patient in the bed. She stirs, the small bump under the covers shifting and then turning into a little girl as her head emerges from the blankets. Her hair is fine, soft strands of silk floating up around her head, charged with static. Huge blue eyes filled with panic fix on me and begin to fill with tears.

Her tiny bottom lip wobbles. "Where's Mason?" she asks.

I clip her chart to the end of her bed again and go and sit beside her on the edge of the mattress. She's so small, even for her age. Her fingers clasp at the blankets that cover her, clutching them to her fragile frame. She looks like a doll. It breaks my heart that such a delicate, innocent child has to suffer through such pain and worry. "Mason's coming soon, sweetheart," I tell her. "He had to go to work, but he promised he would come as soon as he was finished. He should be here in about an hour or so."

Tears fall from both of her eyes at the same time, racing each other down her cheeks. "He doesn't normally leave me," she whispers. "I don't like hospitals."

"Ahh, sweetie. You want me to let you in on a little secret?" I lean a little closer to her, smiling a little. I never wanted to work with kids. The peds rotation in med school was challenging to say the least; I could handle most heartbreak you encounter in hospitals, but terminally ill children were just too much for me. As I look at Millie now, I can see the same shadow hanging over her that hung over those little babies, and it feels as though my throat is swelling shut. Millie nods, gripping her blankets tighter.

"I hate hospitals, too," I whisper.

Her eyes grow even rounder. "But you're a doctor. You can't hate hospitals."

I shrug, looking up at the ceiling. "I like helping

people. That's why I became a doctor. But I don't like hospitals. You know, my daddy is a doctor just like me. And when I was little, I never saw him. He was always working, always coming home so late, when I was already tucked up and asleep in bed, and I used to get so angry with him for spending all of his time at the hospital. I used to get mad at all the sick people that wanted him to spend all of his time with them instead of me. It took me a long time to realize that he was doing a very important job and that they needed him more than I did. I realized he still loved me, no matter what, and I would always be his little girl. That never changed how I felt about hospitals, though. I always hated them."

Millie's eyebrows climb upward. "Do you hate being here now?"

"No. Not now. I like being here, talking to you."

With a little wriggle and a grunt, Millie sits up, resting against the mountain of pillows her brother insisted she needed on her bed. "You helped me when I came here earlier, didn't you? I remember this." She reaches up and touches me lightly on the arm, pointing at my watch. "It's very shiny," she whispers. "I think Mason used to have a watch like that one."

My watch, an inexpensive copy of a Rolex, is one of my most valuable possessions. It was given to me by one of my very first patients—a woman I treated with ovarian cancer. I'd been an intern at the time, so she wasn't even my patient, but I'd been the one to diagnose her. The doctor presiding over her case, Dr. Withers, had insisted she had celiac's disease but back then I'd had the same nagging, uncomfortable sensation that something wasn't quite right, and I'd investigated further. The tiny mass on her left ovary would have been easy to miss if I hadn't been looking so hard for it. The woman, Casey, had been so grateful that I'd caught the malignant tumor that she'd come back and brought me the watch a couple of weeks after she'd finished her chemo treatments. She'd looked tired, with large shadows underneath her eyes, but she'd been given the all clear. She was cancer free, and she said she had me to thank for that.

Casey and I kept in touch for a long time. She'd send me pictures of her daughter, telling me about all of the milestones she'd been able to witness in her child's life. After a while the letters stopped, though. A couple of years into my residency, I learned that Casey had died from a secondary bout of ovarian cancer that had snuck back in and taken root. By the time they started treating her, it was already too late.

"You like it?" I show Millie the reflective glass face, marked with years of use and abuse in St. Peter's of Mercy Hospital. She nods. Quickly, I unclip the strap and slide the watch onto her rail-thin arm, fastening it as tightly as I can. "Do you think you could look after it for me while you're here? I keep banging it on things."

Millie studies the watch for a second, her tiny index finger tracing over the scratches and scuffs on the glass, and then she nods again. "I'll look after it for you," she says. "I'll give it back when Mason takes me home."

"Thank you, Millie. I'd like that."

••••

Dr. Bochowitz isn't exactly a rule breaker, but the old guy knows when not to ask questions. He doesn't seem to find it out of the ordinary at all that I might want to house a six-year-old patient in the morgue. Millie doesn't seem to be bothered by the lack of natural lighting or the strange chemical smell that permeates the room, either. In fact, she seems quite comfortable in her new surroundings, away from the hustle and bustle of nurses running through the corridors and people coding around her twenty-four seven. Bochowitz makes sure all of the bodies he was working on are securely locked away before she can lay eyes on them, and then he brings her some dinner and sits with her as she eats, telling her stories about his granddaughter, who is apparently the same age as Millie.

I wait for Mason to arrive upstairs on the trauma floor, hoping a horrific car accident is brought in so I don't have to explain to the guy that his little sister is now safe and sound downstairs in the morgue. The poor kid's probably going to have nightmares for years.

No natural disaster strikes the city, though, and the roads are free of ten car pile-ups. Mason finds me twenty minutes behind schedule, covered in grease and dirt, looking beyond stressed as he turns his car keys over and over in his hands. "Where is she?" he demands. "I went by her room and the bed was fucking empty. I thought something terrible had happened."

Mason stares at me, wearing a blank expression as I explain what I've done. I can't tell if he's happy I've found a work-around of sorts, or if he's really mad that Millie is now the only living resident in the St. Peter's morgue. He blinks once, and then blinks again. "Can you take me to her?" he asks.

I do. People sometimes do take the elevator down into the morgue, primarily so they can view the bodies of their dead loved ones and relatives, to say goodbye, but it's not the norm. Mason doesn't seem anywhere near sad enough to be in mourning as we ride down into the sub-level and exit, but the young nurse standing beside him gives him a sad, reassuring smile all the same.

Millie's sitting up and talking to Bochowitz when we enter the room. Her eyes light up when she sees her brother, and Mason's voice catches in his throat as he says hello. "I see you're creating mischief as per usual, little Millie Mouse."

She feigns annoyance, folding her arms across her body. "Am not. Mister Richard was telling me ghost stories. I wasn't even scared, Mase. I listened the whole way through!"

Bochowitz looks a little sheepish as he stands from

his seat by Millie's bed. "Ahh, yes, well I may have gotten a little carried away with my stories as it goes. But I couldn't help myself. Young Miss Reeves here is quite the little lady. Very brave indeed. Seemed like a shame to leave out the exciting parts."

Mason offers out his hand to Dr. Bochowitz, who shakes his in return. "Thanks for watching over her," he says. "And thanks for keeping her entertained. If she has nightmares, I'll be sending her over to your place for you to deal with, though."

"I won't have nightmares," Millie says. "I'm too old for nightmares."

"Everyone has bad dreams sometimes, baby. Even grown ups."

Millie looks stunned by this information. She wriggles down into her pillows and tilts her head to one side. "That's not very fair," she says. "Grown ups shouldn't have to be afraid when they're big."

Mason lets out a shaky laugh, rocking his head from side to side. "Grown ups get scared all the time, I'm sure. All of us. We can just handle it better than little kids, Mill."

The sweet little girl in the bed flares her nostrils as she pulls a giant lungful of air into her body. She looks from Dr. Bochowitz to her brother, and then to me, at which point she shakes her head. "You don't get scared, Mason. You're the bravest brother ever. You're never, *never* afraid of anything."

I can see her wanting to believe this so badly. If Mason never gets scared, then Millie knows her protector is brave and capable of taking care of her. Mason must be all too aware of this, too. He chucks her under the chin, grinning. "Fair enough. You caught me. I don't scare easy, that's for sure."

I know the truth, though. Mason, like anyone in charge of another person's wellbeing, especially a child, is scared all the time. If he's like any of the other parents who walk the hallways of St. Peter's, he's paralyzed by fear. He does a good job of hiding it in front of Millie, though.

"When can we go home?" Millie tries to throw back her covers, as though she's ready this instant. She's thwarted by the tightly tucked in sheets, so she doesn't make it far.

"Soon, baby. We just need to—" He stops short as his phone starts ringing loudly in his pocket. "Shit. I'm sorry. I know I'm supposed to switch that off." He fishes his cell phone out of his pocket, and his expression darkens as he looks at the screen.

Bochowitz waves off his apology. "That's okay, Mr. Reeves. As you can see normal rules don't apply down here. Feel free to answer that if you need to. You can step out into the hallway."

Mason shoots him a rueful smile, nodding his head. "Thanks. Unfortunately I do have to take this call." Getting to his feet, his eyes meet mine as he moves past me to exit through the door; I couldn't work it out before, how he felt about me moving Millie down here, out of sight, but now I can see the gratitude in his eyes. Thank fuck for that. He could easily report me to the Chief, and that would be me finished. Bochowitz starts talking to Millie again, distracting her while her brother is indisposed. I'm turning, about to join them, when I hear Mason answer his phone. The door is closing quickly behind him, but I still have time to register the first words that come out of his mouth, and I'm chilled to the bone by what I overhear.

"Detective Lowell," he says. "I haven't been able to check in on Mayfair today."

SIX

Mason

Lowell's pissed. She doesn't seem to understand that if I'm at the hospital with my baby sister, I'm not going to be able to do her dirty work for her. She is prickly as fuck as she dresses me down over the phone. "You realize, Mason, that we're working with a time limit here. If I don't find any evidence relating to this murder soon, I won't be able to pursue Mayfair as a person of interest. That's bad for me. Very, very bad, which means it's very, very bad for you, too. And your little sister. I mean, all it would take is one phone call to child services…"

"Fuck. Can you—can you just give me another day or two? I'm doing the best I can, okay? Zeth's a hard man to get a read on. He keeps his cards close to his chest. It's not as if he's spilling his guts about the dead bodies he's buried in the mountains every time we spar. He's not that stupid. He barely knows me."

"You sound like you respect him," Lowell says. "You sound like I'm making you unfairly spy on an innocent man. Remember this, Mason. Men like Zeth are charismatic. They're charming. They lull you into a false sense of security."

"I don't know who the fuck you've had dealings with in the past, but Zeth's not charming or charismatic in the slightest. He's an unfriendly, prickly motherfucker, and I am scared *shitless* of him. I have no sense of security at all, false or otherwise."

Lowell just grunts. "Whatever. You know what the stakes are here, Mason. Get him talking."

"I don't know how to do that! I'm not a fucking interrogator. I've got no experience with this kind of shit."

"Jesus. Just get him drunk. All men love to boast about the shit they've done when they've got a gallon of Jack Daniels inside them."

This woman has no idea what she's asking of me. If she does, then she obviously doesn't give a shit about my personal wellbeing. In the brief time I've known Denise Lowell, she doesn't strike me as the kind of person to allow other people's safety to get in the way of what she wants, though.

"I'll do my best," I tell her. "That's all I can do."

"Bullshit like that is for five-year-olds and losers, Mr.

Reeves. Do better than your best. Do *my* best. Do whatever it takes." The line goes dead, and I'm left standing in
the hallway with my cell phone still pressed against my
ear, wondering how the fuck I got myself dragged into
this mess.

I head back into the room and find Millie counting off
her best friends on what looks like both her hands and
both her feet. The old guy doctor is good with her, I have
to admit that. He puts up a good front, showing interest
in who Octavia, Rosie and Samantha are. Dr. Romera, on
the other hand, is wearing a sharp, hostile look on her
face that I recognize all too well. I was wearing it earlier
when she was trying to convince me to keep Millie at St.
Peter's. If looks could kill, I'd be hanged, drawn and
quartered and already buried six feet under.

"Is everything okay, Dr. Romera?"

She jumps, as if we haven't been staring at each other
since I walked back into the room and she's only just
noticed me now. "Yes. Yeah. Everything is fine," she says.
Her voice is flat, though. Cold. It's as if she's a different
person, all of a sudden gone is the warm, caring, friendly
doctor I was dealing with a moment ago, and in her
place stands...I don't even know who she is now.
"Everything is perfect," she says, unfolding her arms
from across her chest and placing her hands slowly into
the pockets of her white lab coat. "I'm afraid you'll have
to excuse me for a moment, guys. It's my turn to make an
important phone call." She gives me another frosty,

appraising look, and then flashes a perfunctory smile at her colleague. "You won't mind if I step away for a moment?"

Dr. Bochowitz grabs one of my sister's toes through the sheets and tugs on it playfully. "Of course not. There's nowhere I would rather be."

Dr. Romera leaves. It feels like she wants to run out of the room, but she's doing her best to walk instead. A cold chill runs up and down my spine. What the fuck is up with her? What could possibly have happened during the time I left the room? Doesn't make any goddamn sense. I swear, I will never understand women.

••••

Millie falls asleep around nine. I feel like shit for leaving her again after being gone all day, but my hope is she'll sleep through and won't miss me until morning. I thought about calling Ben and canceling my fight tonight, but we need the money. Desperately. If I don't fight, I'm two grand down, and that's our rent money for the month. That's money I need to pay our utilities and put food on the table for Millie. It won't be anywhere near enough to cover the bills we've racked up at the hospital—I'll have to fight again next week to even come close to settling those, which makes me worried. If I don't win, if I get injured, if Millie's ill again and I can't leave her...

I'm plagued by ifs.

The night air is cool as I climb into my car and head south, out of the city toward La Maison Markets. French's, an enclosed, dusty, airless storage facility under the markets, will already be thrumming, alive with crowds of people expecting to see blood tonight. They're bankers and stockbrokers, baggage handlers, mechanics, nannies and chefs. They're everyone, you and me, people from all walks of life. They're the people of Seattle unafraid to show their true colors, to cast their money hand over fist as they bay for violence and carnage. They are how I keep the devil from my door, though most of the time they somehow make me feel like I *am* the devil.

I park up and head down the narrow staircase that leads into the basement where the fights take place, my head still back at the hospital with Millie. I'm third on the card tonight. I haven't lost a single fight yet, but I'm still not the main event. There are other fighters, favorites who've been kicking the shit out of people way longer than I have, that still claim the title fight. They're earning upwards of twenty grand a match if they're good negotiators, and the guy fighting tonight is that and more. *Jameson Rayne*. He's notorious for his round one knock outs. His right hook is fucking terrifying. You see that thing coming and that's it. No time for blocking. No counter on earth is good enough to prevent a serious concussion and a few missing teeth. Only the maddest of the mad take on Rayne. Only people like Ben.

My best friend greets me out the back, where a hot blonde with gigantic fake tits is stroking her hand up and down his bicep like he's some kind of fucking demi god. When he looks up and sees me, he slaps the chick on the ass and sends her packing.

"She won't be so eager to bounce up and down on your dick later, when you're black and blue and humiliated, asshole," I tell him.

Ben smirks. "So what? My dick's chaffed raw from her bouncing up and down on it already. I need some time to recover. There'll be another chick just like her ready to ride my cock in a couple of weeks, and I'll *still* be flush from this fight."

He's right. Rayne may make a shit load of cash from thrashing Ben tonight, but that's not to say Ben will be going home empty handed. Everyone knows there's no chance they'll win against Rayne. It requires a decent purse to entice fighters to come and take the beating of their lives, and tonight it's Ben's turn to get thrown around the cage. Crazy bastard.

"You given any more thought to what we talked about?" he asks, holding up his hand wraps. I take them from him and begin to wind them around his right hand.

"No. You know I can't leave, man. If there was any way…" A few weeks ago, Ben mentioned that he's thinking about moving to LA to train with the pros and he hasn't fucking let up about it since.

"They have schools in California, dickwad. They have

auto mechanic shops, too."

"It's not that simple. Millie's settled here. She's got friends. I'd be screwed if Wanda didn't pick up Millie from school every day. I wouldn't be able to work." I don't mention that I have a DEA agent shoved so far up my ass, she knows exactly what I ate for breakfast. If I try to leave the state, Lowell will have CPS on my doorstep quicker than I can blink.

Ben flexes his hand when I finish wrapping him, easing the material around his knuckles so he can still form a fist. "All I'm saying is Los Angeles is where we need to be if we want to start making any headway in this industry. You know it, and I know it. If we stay here, fighting for chump change every weekend of the year, we're never gonna end up on cards in Vegas. Joe Rogan ain't gonna be talking about us on his podcast. This will be it for us. Until Jameson Rayne finally gets knocked the fuck out and makes room for the rest of us, we'll always be playing second fiddle."

I don't give a shit about playing second fiddle. I'm not trying to build a career for myself here. I wouldn't be fighting at all if I didn't have Millie to take care of. Ben doesn't understand this, because he's young and he has no fucking responsibilities. I may be the same age as him, but I'm fifteen years ahead of him in the dependent stakes, and there's nothing I can do about that. Every decision I make, every single action, every last move— it's all for her, and it will be until the day I die.

"Whatever, man." I wrap his other hand while he tries, yet again, to tell me how easy it would be to get a job in LA. How kids Millie's age always make new friends easy. It's only when he starts bullshitting about how the hospitals are so much better in Cali and Millie would get better treatment out there that I cut him off.

"Look, dude, I just can't. I'm sorry. Not right now. Maybe in a year or two. I'm sorry." Ben can tell from my tone of voice that this is the end of our conversation on the topic. He sighs, thumping his fist into his palm, disappointment rolling off him.

"All right, Mase. But fuck. A year or two's a long time in the UFC. I don't know if I can hang around that long."

"You should go," I tell him. "Fuck, go and make your name, man. I don't wanna be the one keeping you here. You don't owe me anything."

Ben grumbles. "You're such an asshole. If you said don't go, wait for my ass to be ready, then I'd get mad at you and go. But when you say that shit instead, there's no way I can leave."

He's fucking ridiculous. He makes no sense half the fucking time. I punch him in the gut, hard enough that he doubles over, groaning melodramatically. "If you want me to suck your dick, man, it ain't gonna happen," I tell him.

Ben howls with laughter. "I already told you, my dick's chaffed right now. Maybe after I beat Rayne I'll hit you up for some victory head, though."

SEVEN

Mason

I win my fight, but not without getting my bell rung pretty hard. The guy I'm matched against is a seasoned vet, and I make the mistake of believing he's flagging in the third round. I get cocky in the fourth, dropping my guard to showcase a little, trying to rile up the crowd some, and that's when the bastard smashes his fist into the side of my head, right where my jaw bone connects with my skull. They call that the button. The off switch. Get hit hard enough right there and it's lights out, motherfucker. Thankfully I manage to feint to the left a little, which lessens his blow, otherwise I'd be counting stars and my ass would be hitting the canvas. I stagger back, slamming into the chain link of the cage, and my head starts swimming.

I needed the reality check. I needed to feel the panic

that comes with the realization that I might actually lose this fight. It spurs me on, fills me with the anger I need to come back swinging. I take the fucker out at the end of the round, sending him crashing to the ground like falling timber. Most of the time, practiced fighters are on the look out for pile-driver hooks and uppercuts from new guys like me, but they're not as prepared for back kicks and roundhouses. The crowd screams in disbelief as I plant my foot, pivot and land a powerful kick to the side of his head, knocking him clean out, and that's it. That's all she wrote.

Predictably, Ben gets his ass handed to him in the first round. The crowd loves seeing him sail through the air, falling like a bundle of limp, wet rags onto the canvas as his lights go out. Rayne's a decent sportsman, crouching down beside Ben and waiting until he regains consciousness before he gets up to celebrate, fist pumping and hollering at the masses of people packed around the cage, who chant his name and rattling the chain link, going wild.

I catch the flash of white-blonde hair by the entrance to the cage and I do my best to get the fuck out of there before the owner of the unmistakable pixie cut catches me, but I'm not quick enough. The crowds move out of the way as hurriedly as they can for me, bodies jostling against bodies, people standing on one another's feet as I slip through them, but they magically part for Kaya Rayne like she's the queen of fucking Sheba. Her hand is on my shoulder before I can get halfway to the exit.

"Smooth," she purrs. "And here I was, thinking we were friends."

I turn and there she stands—perfectly formed, pocketsize Kaya, with her rosebud mouth and devilish twinkle in her pale blue eyes. Damn. I've been hiding from her for weeks like a goddamn coward. What the fuck is wrong with me? She's smoking hot. As far as I can tell, she's very interested in seeing me naked, which is awesome because I find myself imagining what her nipples look like, how they'd feel in my mouth, at least three or four times a day. Don't get me started on how much time I spend thinking about her pussy. I should be giving her exactly what she wants: my dick. And yet I can't. It wouldn't be even close to fair. My life is a fucking circus right now. To drag her into it would be shitty beyond measure.

"Hey. What's up?" I rub the back of my neck, scanning the sea of people pressing in around us, trying to see Ben. If I can find him, I'll be able to use him as an excuse—the old, *I-gotta-go-take-care-of-my-friend* bit. Kaya seems to have other ideas, though.

"Hmm. What's up? Well, lately I've been worried about how complicated technology is getting, y'know?"

"I'm sorry?" Her weird response throws me off balance.

"Yeah, you know. Old people can't work TV remotes anymore. People in their forties can't figure out social media apps. Now it seems like guys in their mid-twenties don't even know how to use their cell phones to reply to their text messages."

Ahhh. That makes more sense. She's pissed at me. "God, Kaya. I'm sorry. I've just been kinda tied up the past few weeks."

"Literally or figuratively?" She reaches into the pocket of her jacket and pulls something out of it, the end of which goes straight into her mouth. A red vine. The girl seems to have a never-ending supply of the damned things.

"Figuatively," I answer. "Of course not literally."

"Okay, 'cause, see, even when people are really busy they still find time to shoot other people a quick text message. It happens all the time. So I asked because I figured, Kaya, give him the benefit of the doubt. Maybe he actually *was* hog tied in someone's basement, and he was only released from captivity earlier this afternoon."

Ben's nowhere to be seen. Fucking Ben. He's probably bleeding profusely in the showers by now and I could really use an out. "It just didn't seem fair," I say. "I don't have time for a relationship, Kaya. I like you, I do, but if we hooked up it would only be sex. And I don't want you to think I'm using you."

"Why?" She snaps some red vine off in between her teeth and chews, frowning up at me.

"Why what?"

"Why don't you want to use me for sex? Am I

repulsive or something?"

Oh god. How the fuck am I supposed to answer *that* without putting a foot wrong? "You're beautiful. You know you are. You *know* I wanna fuck you. I just don't want to *hurt* you."

Looking around, Kaya laughs quietly down her nose. She doesn't look hurt. In fact, she looks amused. "You can't hurt me, sweetheart. You want to fuck me. I want to fuck you. We both want to use each other for sex. So we should."

I just stare at her. Believe it or not, I've been in this position before. Girls have used this line on me in the past, given me the whole, 'I don't want anything from you story,' and then two months down the line they're trying to sleep over at your place every night and attempting to introduce you to their parents. It never ends well. When Kaya says it, though, I get the impression I'd be the one trying to sleep over at her place every night, attempting to talk her into meeting my parents. I guess there's no real fear of that happening, since both my mother and father are long dead, but still... Kaya makes me feel like I'm not the one in control here, and I don't fucking like it. It's terrifying. I've never liked a girl enough to consider picturing where she might slot into my life on a permanent basis. I don't think Kaya *would* slot into my life. I get the feeling everything would have to change to accommodate her, and that just can't happen. It's just not possible.

Kaya sucks the red vine into her mouth, wrapping her lips around the twisted red candy, and my dick stirs in my pants. She knows all too well what she's doing. It's a cheap and obvious trick, but it's also really fucking effective. My mind instantly starts showing me how awesome it would be if she were sucking my cock instead of that length of licorice, and she waggles her eyebrows, trying not to grin.

"You need to loosen up, Reeves. Not everything has to be serious. Sometimes, things can just be *fun*." Slowly, she begins to back away, melting into the crowd, and I'm painfully fucking aware of the fact that I'm still in the tight shorts I fought in, and I'm about to be sporting an obvious boner. "If you remember how to use that cell phone of yours, you should reply to one of my texts. I'd love to help you relax sometime soon." She gives me a tiny wave, and then she vanishes, swallowed by the surging flood of people now trying to leave French's since the fights are over with.

Someone slaps me on the back. Another guy in a pale grey suit with a dark wet stain down the lapel hands me a fifty-dollar bill and laughs like a hyena as he tells me I won him three grand tonight. More people thank me, congratulate me, and shake my hand, but I don't really hear the words coming from their mouths. All I'm thinking about is Kaya Rayne's mouth wrapped around that red vine. Kaya Rayne's mouth wrapped around my dick.

God damn, that woman is dangerous.

••••

I am electric, alive, filled from head-to-toe with an exhausted energy as I jog across the parking lot toward the truck. By rights I should be exhausted after a long, stressful day like today, but fighting always does this to me. If I were in bed with a woman right now, I could fuck for hours. I could come over and over again and it wouldn't matter. This kind of buzz doesn't dissipate at the drop of a hat. It lingers, keeps your mind sharp, honing your senses so you're aware of everything. I'm considering driving straight back to St. Peter's, foregoing sleep altogether, but then my mind flashes white, all thought vanishing instantly as I notice the black Camaro parked up beside my truck. I'd know that Camaro anywhere; I see it every day, pulling up outside the Blood & Roses Fighting Gym.

What the *fuck* is Zeth doing here? He knows about the underground cage fights that take place at French's, he must, everyone does, but I never expected to see him here. No way.

I slow my jog down to a walk, my heart suddenly thumping out of rhythm, spiking, shock waves of adrenalin rushing my head and my arms, skin tingling. There's no such thing as luck in this world, either good or bad. It's no happy coincidence that the crazy bastard from across the street has somehow managed to come

75

across my truck and has accidentally parked beside it, when the rest of the parking lot is fucking empty. No, he's been waiting for me here for god knows how long, and I really don't want to find out why.

No good trying to slink off into the shadows now, though. He must have seen me, the same way I've seen him. I'm condemning myself if I bolt. I try to loosen the stiffness that's settled in my shoulders as I walk directly to the driver's side window of the Camaro, already planning out what I'm going to say to him.

'Oh, hey, man.' (Insert enigmatic smile here.) *'You came to the fights? D'you see Jameson Rayne destroy Ben Farminger in the first round? Crazy, right?'*

Or…

'Hey, Zeth. What brings you out to the Markets on this fine evening? Couldn't sleep?'

When I reach his window and the glass slides down, though, I don't say a word. Inside the front seat, Zeth sits as still as a statue, staring straight ahead out of his windscreen, one hand resting on the steering wheel, the other resting on the Camaro's gear stick. He doesn't look at me. He doesn't breathe a word.

He knows.

I exhale, letting my head hang, my chin nearly hitting my chest. Zeth starts the Camaro's engine, and I know what's expected of me. Fuck Lowell. Fuck this whole day. Fuck my fucking life. I go around and climb into the front passenger seat beside him; Zeth throws the car into gear as soon as my ass is in the seat and the door is closed behind me. The inside of the car smells like lemon and leather soap, like it's just been detailed.

"She threatened to take her away," I say quietly. "I couldn't let her do that, man. Millie's been through enough. She's just a kid."

Zeth grunts, eyes still fixed on an unknown point in the road. I don't expect kindness or understanding from a man like him. His reputation precedes him. He's a cold-blooded killer. Lowell wouldn't be chasing him down so hard if she weren't one hundred percent sure he is responsible for the death of the girl on the mountain. So perhaps this is how it ends: me being driven off into the night, my sister still in the hospital, destined to wake up tomorrow, wondering where the fuck I am. Maybe I'm about to give Lowell the evidence she needs to put Mayfair away once and for all. Zeth could be driving me out into the wilds, where he's already found the perfect spot to dump my freshly dead body into a freshly dug grave. All I know is I'm in big, big fucking trouble, and there's no way out of it now.

EIGHT

Zeth

There are only a few rules I live by. I can count them on one hand. First: if you're going to kill a man, make sure he's definitely dead before you dispose of the body. Second: Always check every room for a potential threat when you enter an empty house. Third: If something seems too good to be true, it definitely fucking is. Lastly, fourth: never snitch on someone, no matter how fucking terrible they are. *Ever*.

It was never an option to hand Charlie Holsan over to the police. It was never a consideration that I might be able to hand him over to Seattle's boys in blue and let them do their jobs. They might have prosecuted him, finally bringing him to justice for all of the terrible atrocities he committed throughout his life, putting him away forever. Holsan could have spent every last breath he took locked behind bars, his freedom taken away until he finally died in his prison issue cot, his bones aching, crippled with arthritis, but I couldn't have given them the information they needed to make it happen. Fuck no. It's just not how things are done.

Mason Reeves remains still as I drive through the night. I had to come clean when Sloane called and told me what she'd overheard. I had to pick him up and figure this shit out once and for all. Typical that Mason would end up in St. Peter's, and typical that it would have to be *my* girlfriend that treated his sister. The world is just too fucking small sometimes. Sloane was not happy with me at all for keeping Lowell's presence a secret, not happy at all, but she was far more concerned over what I had planned for the guy. She could hear the cold violence in my voice, no doubt. She knew all too well what that meant, and she didn't like it. Took forever to convince her to leave the hospital and go home, to get some sleep and wait for me there, but she'd finally agreed. And now, here I am driving Mason across the city toward the warehouse, wondering how the hell I'm supposed to deal with this situation. I gave up killing people, yes, but shit. I also swore I'll do anything I have to in order to make sure Sloane is safe, no matter fucking what, and let's face it: I'm still so fucking mad at him. I'm so mad I could quite easily lose control and snap his neck.

Mason watches with alert eyes as we head across the

city, moving toward the water and the docklands. I've had grown ass men in the same position as Mason, zip tied and thrown into the trunk of this Camaro, crying their fucking eyes out, and yet the kid just climbed in and hasn't made a peep since. There's something to be said about that.

When we reach the warehouse, Michael's standing in the open doorway, a rectangle of bright light blaring out into the darkness behind him. The deep navy blue suit he's wearing is immaculate as ever. I swear the guy's wardrobe must be worth thousands and thousands of dollars. He opens up Mason's door for him and stands back so he can get out.

"Hey, man," Mason says.

Michael smiles at him, placing a hand on his shoulder. "Better come inside, huh?" He sounds a little sad—bastard's supposed to be on my side, not feeling sorry for the guy who's been feeding information to the woman hell-bent on destroying our lives. I shoot him a dark look, and Michael just shrugs. He's not sorry in the slightest. Some right hand man he's gonna be tonight. I follow them inside the warehouse, pulling the heavy sliding door back into place behind us and locking it shut, and then I make my way into the living room, where I find Sloane sitting on the couch with her hands knotted together, her face as white as a sheet.

"You have got to be fucking kidding me," I growl. "What happened to waiting at home, getting some sleep?" I spin on Michael, ready to punch the traitor in the head. "And you? What the fuck were you thinking, letting her come here?"

Michael arches an eyebrow at me, sighing. "You know your girlfriend better than anyone else, man. If you think there was any element of 'allowing' her to do something here, then you're giving me far too much credit."

"You should have picked her the fuck up and forced her to go home," I snarl.

"I threatened it. Then Sloane helpfully pointed out what you'd do to me if I laid hands on her, and I decided to leave her to her own devices."

I have nothing to say to that. Fair enough, I would have torn him limb from limb if Sloane had been man-handled in any way. Still, though. Fucking unbelievable that he'd just let her waltz in and make herself comfortable on the couch, knowing what's about to happen to this kid.

"You can't be mad at Michael," Sloane says. Her voice is cool, filled with ice water. She's pissed at me—I can see it in her eyes. I don't need to hear her say the words, but still she says them anyway. "You should never have kept me in the dark on this. I should have known about Lowell from the start."

"It could have been nothing," I growl. "What would have been the point in worrying you?"

She glares at me with the intensity of a thousand suns. Not another word comes out of her mouth, but I can tell this matter is far from resolved.

"I can come back later if you like?" Mason says, jerking his thumb over his shoulder. Smart ass.

I give him a look that makes the small smile slide right off his face. "Just sit the fuck down."

He obeys, sitting down opposite Sloane. He gives her a barely visible nod of the head. "So you guys know each other. I guess this explains why you were so frosty when I came back into the room earlier," he says. "I had no idea. I'm really sorry, Dr. Romera."

Sloane clears her throat. She looks around the room, before she finally lets her gaze rest on the kid. "I had no idea you were training with Zeth, either. Tell us about Lowell. Why are you helping her? And what does she want to know?"

She's asked the burning question we've been trying to figure out ever since I laid eyes on Lowell again. Sloane has also asked another question I probably wouldn't have bothered with: what were Mason's motives for helping her? See, this is the difference between a person like Sloane, a *normal* person, and a person like me. She cares about the *why*. She gives a shit about the reasoning behind someone's actions. I don't care about that. I only care about Mason's betrayal, right alongside the consequences of that betrayal.

Mason rubs the back of his neck, shaking his head. "She knew about Millie. She said she was going to have her taken away if I didn't help her. She wanted me to find out if Zeth ever went up into the mountains. One specific place. They found a body buried up there. Some dog walker's Lab was going nuts, digging in the dirt. A nearby river flooded in all the rain we had a couple of weeks ago, and a body was unearthed. When forensics did their thing, they found a partial print that belonged to Zeth. That's all I know."

My stomach muscles clench tight, as if I've just been sucker punched hard to the gut. What the fuck is he talking about? A body buried by a river in the mountains? A partial print? Of course, I know exactly what the fuck he's talking about, but I don't want to admit it to myself. This can't be happening. Just fucking *can't*. Less than a few months ago, we buried a body up there in the mountains, but we buried her deep. We buried her in the most secluded spot we could find, where she would be at peace, where she wouldn't have to suffer any further.

We didn't count on the floodwaters loosening the soil, though. There was no way to know the storms that hit Seattle recently would unearth her, disrupting her final resting place.

Sloane and Michael exchange a wary look. They both know what this means, too. They found my sister. They found Lacey.

Sloane

I've seen Zeth angry before, too many times to recall, but

this time it's different. This time his anger is tinged with a pain he usually tries to tamp down and forget about, but now he's being forced to face it head on, and it's more than he can bear. My beautiful, wild Zeth. Still so torn apart inside by grief that he can't even say his sister's name. I'm still mad at him, yes, but I'm also hurting so bad for him right now.

"No doubt they found more than a partial print on her," Michael's saying somewhere in the distance. "We all touched her. Every last one of us helped lower her into the ground."

"I'm the only one with a criminal record. My fingerprints are the only ones in their database." He sounds stunned. None of us ever thought we'd be faced with this problem. We've tiptoed around the subject of Lacey because no one really wants to deal with the fresh, brightly burning pain of her loss yet. Not even me, who knew her so briefly. I loved her, though. It was impossible not to. The indignity of her body being dug up by a Labrador is significant; it feels as though we've disrespected her in the worst way, allowing her remains to be now poked and prodded at by a forensic team as well.

"And so Lowell just somehow managed to find out about this and came back here?" I say. "It makes no sense. This isn't her jurisdiction. A murder has nothing to do with drugs. Not necessarily, anyway."

Mason says, "She said she has homicides in this area

flagged. She thinks they're all linked to some motorcycle gang over in New Mexico who deal weed."

Zeth laughs bitterly. "The Widow Makers don't deal weed. Maybe they used to run it from state to state every once in a while, but not in a long ass time."

For a moment, we all sit in silence, mulling on the information we've just received. Lowell's trying to pin Lacey's murder on Zeth. Ironic that he's killed a fair few people in his time and yet Lacey, the one person he didn't kill, is potentially going to mean trouble for him. Perhaps Lowell knows Zeth isn't responsible for Lacey's death, and perhaps she doesn't. Either way, she'll bend every rule and limbo under red tape until she finds a way to make the charge stick.

"What have you told her?" Zeth demands, crossing the room toward Mason. The kid leans back into his chair, eyes full of steel, jaw set. He's determined not to show fear.

"I told her about Michael," he says. "I said I thought he was probably doing a lot of your dirty work for you."

Michael laughs. "*Charming.*"

"I don't know, man. I had to tell her something. She's convinced something illegal's going on at the gym, like you might be dealing drugs or guns there or something. She told me to stick around after hours as often as I could and eavesdrop on any meetings you might have."

"And how did that work out for you?" Zeth's lips are pressed together, turned white from the pressure he's applying to them. This version of him is an echo, a ghost of the man he was when we first met. He's still so shut off sometimes, so stern and stoic when interacting with the outside world, but he's a million times better than he used to be. The wall that stood between him and the rest of society has been deconstructed for a while now; it's strange and unpleasant to see it go back up again so easily now.

"I told her the truth—that you don't have meetings there. She didn't believe me, though. She wanted me to stay later. Go over there every day. She'd know if I didn't show up. That's why she called today. She knew I was at the hospital instead of at the gym."

"And where does she think you are now?" Zeth asks.

Mason rubs his chin with his fingertips. "Who the fuck knows. She'll know I'm not at the gym, and I'm sure she'll know I'm not with Millie. She'll probably think you've figured me out and you're about to murder my ass," he says, glaring accusingly at up Zeth.

God, if he's trying to ingratiate himself with the man, he's really not doing a great job. He has a point, though. "Why don't you just take Mason back to the hospital?" I have no reason to think Zeth will listen to me, he rarely does, but it would be better for everyone involved if he does just this once. "Lowell wouldn't expect you to let Mason go if you were to find out that he's been watching you for her. She'll expect you to hurt him and make him disappear. Take him back to the hospital and she'll be none the wiser."

"Sloane's right," Michael adds. "That way we could use him to feed her the information we want her to know and nothing else."

"And have him coming into the gym every day? Around you and now my fucking girlfriend? I don't think so."

"So what? You're going to kill him? Right in front of me? You're not even going to consider sparing a stupid kid's life? He was only acting to protect his sister, Zeth."

Mason's eyes flash with anger—he clearly doesn't like being called a stupid kid—but he refrains from saying anything. Probably the smartest thing he's done since he walked into the room. Zeth turns his full attention on me for the first time since he walked in with Mason.

"You're the one who told me what he'd done, Sloane. You're the one who called me the moment you heard him on the phone with Lowell."

"I know. I was worried about the DEA, though. I was worried about your safety. Turns out this wasn't a fresh, pressing issue. You've known about it for a while. And I never wanted you to hurt him, Zeth." I take a deep breath, knowing my next argument is going to either fall flat or make him flip out. I have to say it, though. I don't want Mason dead and in pieces, floating in the Sound just because he had the misfortune to be caught up in our nightmare through no choice of his own. "Think about it," I say. "Really think hard about what you would have done for Lacey, Zeth. Wouldn't you have made a deal with the devil in order to keep her safe? What would you do now to bring her back? You'd bargain with Lowell. You'd bargain with anyone and everyone, and you know it. So let Mason go. Let him take care of his sister, and we'll work out this Lowell thing on our own. It's the best way. It's the best way for all of us."

Zeth stares at the wall. Specifically, he stares at a small, framed picture of a seaside boardwalk that seemingly has no bearing or relationship to Seattle whatsoever. I've thought about that picture a lot; there are other pictures on the walls in the warehouse, but they all seem to be contemporary art pieces. Swooshes and slashes of color, running into each other, over-lapping and contradicting. This photograph, complete with its masses of people crowding the boardwalk, vendors selling hotdogs, arcade in the background, sign lit up despite the stark, pale wash of the blue sky overhead, is the only sentimental object of its kind. Zeth looks away.

"Lowell won't just *stop* calling him," he says. "She won't just forget that he's her inside source. It's not as easy as letting him go so he can take care of his sister, Sloane."

"Then, shit, I don't know. Why don't you tell him what you want him to say to her? That way she thinks she's getting what she needs, and Mason's in the clear. There's a way to manage the situation without anyone dying."

"I, for one, like the sound of that plan," Mason adds.

On the sidelines, literally at the very edge of the room, Michael keeps his own council. I have no idea which plan he thinks is more beneficial over the other, but he watches the scene unfolding before him with sharp, intelligent eyes, the slightest glimmer of curiosity flickering over his features. Mason doesn't even spare the man a sideways glance; he must know his fate rests solely in Zeth's hands. He's the one who decides whether Mason lives or dies. In the past, I know how Zeth would have handled this. He would never have listened to the woman he was sleeping with. He would have shut down the threat without a second thought and moved on to deal with Lowell herself, and there would have been no debate. Things are different now, though. After everything we've been through, Zeth knows I'm not just some naïve, uninformed girl that makes decisions on a whim, without any real thought.

He cracks his index finger knuckle, followed by his middle finger and then he stops. "Fine."

That's all he says. I'm waiting for him to follow up his one word response with a list of caveats, as well as a series of threats that would make even the most hardened criminal's hair stand on end. He leaves it at that, though. He wants to go; I can see how badly he wants to smash his fist into something right now, and he's undoubtedly feeling robbed of the opportunity.

Mason slowly, cautiously gets to his feet. "So I'm good to go?"

Zeth grunts. He jerks his head toward the door, his face stony and unimpressed. "You'd better, before I change my fucking mind."

Animals, unsure whether it's safer to run or safer to flee, will often freeze in place, not breathing, unbelieving, while they try to decide what their best course of action is. Mason is just like one of those animals, a rabbit in the headlights, as he no doubt tries to figure out if Zeth means what he's saying or not. The stupid kid should be dashing for the door, and instead he's standing in the middle of the room with his shoulders hunched, glancing from one person to the next.

"Are you waiting for an Uber?" Michael asks. "If you are, might I suggest you wait outside on the street? Maybe a few blocks from here? We have a slight health and safety issue here right now. And by that, I mean lingering here any longer than you need to is very bad for *your* health and *your* safety."

"Understood." Mason ducks out of the room and heads to the exit of the warehouse, not wasting another second. Zeth stares at the wall again. He flinches when the sound of the sliding metal door slams home, sending clanging echoes through the warehouse.

"I swear I'll never understand why we just let that happen," he comments. "At some point that kid is ending up in a shallow grave at the side of the road. It's inevitable. He has no idea how this world works. *Why* it works the way it does."

"He shouldn't have to. He should just be able to take care of his family, and go to work. Instead, he has to deal with Denise Lowell, and all because he's an easy target. She knows he has access to you, and she knows she can manipulate him. Do you think that's fair?"

Zeth moves subtly, angling his body so that his torso and his hips are facing me. He won't look me in the eye, though. At least he doesn't, until he's just about to vanish through the doorway, into the bowels of the house. "Nothing about life is fair, Sloane. If it were, serial killers and rapists would be riddled with ball cancer and charity workers would be winning the fucking lottery every week. Mason's lucky. If I was Charlie Holsan, there's no way he'd have just walked out of here in tact. He'd have had his throat slit and two guys would be in the process of burning off his fingerprints and pulling his fucking molars out of his head." He doesn't hang back to see what I might have to say to this. He storms off, out of sight, growling darkly under his breath.

"Isn't that the whole point, though?" I yell after him. "*Isn't the whole point that you're* not *Charlie Holsan?*"

NINE

Sloane

Morning light pours through the vast expanse of glass that forms the right hand wall of my bedroom. Miles away, Seattle is a faint blue smudge on the horizon, banded by the gunmetal grey of water in the far distance. The hour is early, must only be five-thirty, six, perhaps, and I'm gripped by the desperate need to pee.

I get up, flinging back the covers, unsurprised by the fact that the other side of my bed is still empty. Zeth slept at the warehouse last night. I gave him the space he needed, though what *I* needed was something else entirely. I needed reassurance and a strong pair of arms around me, holding me tight. I needed to be told I hadn't just made the gravest of errors when I talked him out of killing Mason. Zeth didn't agree with what I had asked of him, though; he was hardly going to be the one to comfort me and tell me everything is going to be okay, when he clearly believes otherwise.

I reach the bathroom just in time. It feels like my bladder's about to explode, and my head right along with it. Man, I feel shitty. I feel worse than when I was gripped in the same flu bug half of St. Peter's is now suffering through. Sure enough, when I try to stand up, the room spins like crazy, pitching and see-sawing, and without warning my stomach rolls. "Shit." I drop down, managing to gather my hair off to one side just in the nick of time before I throw up, last night's paltry dinner of cream cheese on toast making an unpleasant come back, spattering into the toilet bowl.

God, please, no. Please don't say I've managed to catch a different strain of this thing. I wait there, hunched over the porcelain, waiting, biding my time, just in case I'm not done and I'm going to vomit for a second time. I don't, though. My stomach muscles spasm, complaining bitterly as I get to my feet, but I seem to feel a little better. Could have been a one off, after all. It might not be the flu bug, returned with a vengeance to kick my ass. The antibiotics I took for my chest infection seemed to clear everything right up. More likely the cream cheese that's been sitting in my refrigerator for weeks has finally upped and turned bad. I make a mental note to clear out the whole icebox in the next few days as I head back to the bedroom and swing myself back into bed. It's a work day, but I'm not on shift until this afternoon.

Better to rest and get as much sleep as I can before the madness of St. Peter's later on. It's a Friday—the emergency room is going to be packed full of drunks and reprobates, and I'm going to need every lick of strength I can muster to get myself through the night.

I fall asleep immediately, my dreams heavy and intense, pressing in on me. I'm aware of the fact that I'm dreaming as I shift through the bizarre landscape of my unconsciousness, the way you might slip from room to room in a familiar yet almost forgotten house, turning all the door handles, trying to find the way out. It feels like many hours have passed when I wake later, covered in sweat, wrapped tight in the bed sheets, but the clock on the bedside table only reads eight fifteen. Downstairs, the sound of the kettle boiling lets me know Zeth is home. Zeth Mayfair, making himself a pot of coffee. How very domesticated of him. I still have to pinch myself sometimes; it's strange imagining him here with me, living in this house, amongst my things, sleeping in my bed, cooking in my kitchen. Just existing here alongside me. It seems as though it shouldn't be possible, in truth. Men like Zeth don't settle. They don't live out the white picket fence fantasy, reading the paper on a Sunday morning and walking the dog. They're more likely to spear you straight through the heart with your white picket fence post and kidnap Fido.

Speaking of which…

Ernie, professional chaser of dust motes, purveyor of

94

half-chewed socks, skids down the hallway, claws clacking on the polished floorboards as he slides past the open bedroom door, and barrels down the stairs onto the first floor, obviously having heard his master's arrival as well. He yips and pants loudly down there, his claws still clacking as he assaults the man in the kitchen with kisses.

"All right, all right. Damn it, dog. Give me a minute." Zeth sounds grumpy, but I know him all too well. He'll be bending down to the tufty haired schnauzer, ruffling his fur and scrubbing him all over his body, letting him jump up to lick at his jaw and his neck. "You're crazy, you know that?" I hear him say.

I'm about to get up and go down there myself when the stairs begin to creak, accompanied by the sound of heavy boots on antique Maplewood. I don't know why, but I immediately pretend I'm still asleep. *Pathetic.*

Zeth enters the bedroom. I hear him put something down on his side of the bed, and then something on my side, too. The rich smell of coffee fills my senses. "Hey." He touches me, placing his hand lightly on my bare shoulder. "You're so bad at that, you know." I crack one eye open at him. There's a tiny smile on his face. "You screw your eyelids shut really tight. I can tell you're awake the moment I look at you."

"Is that so? Well, maybe I've just been rudely awakened by a really loud intruder, and I'm trying to go back to sleep."

"Are you?" He cocks his head to one side.

"No."

"Then drink your coffee." He's definitely in a better mood than he was last night. Strangely, he appears to be in a *good* mood, which doesn't make all that much sense. Still. I'm not one to argue. I pull myself up so I'm sitting, collecting the mug of tar-black coffee he's brought upstairs for me, and I can smell how sweet it is as I lift it to my lips. Perfection. It's amazing how quickly caffeine can kick start your brain. Zeth watches me drink, his eyes fixed solely on the point where my lips meet the 'Baddest Motherfucker Alive' mug—the one I know he finds hilarious, even though he's never said anything about it.

He doesn't mention last night, or the fact that Mason's now loose, perfectly capable of telling Lowell that we know she's using him as an informant, and there's little we can do about it. Or that it's my fault. He sits on the edge of the bed, looking at me as I drink my coffee, like an artist studies the object of his painting, not expecting me to say anything or comment on the fact that he's observing me. He wants to be an outsider in this moment. He wants to pretend like he's not here, that he's somehow managing to oversee this quiet, simple moment where I relax in bed, taking my time to wake up fully, hair everywhere, weird lines from the pillows marking my neck and my shoulder.

After a while, he says, "I was going to wait."

"Wait for what?"

He's got a flat, impassive look on his face, which usually goes hand in hand with a statement or a parting of information that he knows I'm not going to like. "Wait for you to come home last night. I was gonna wait for you to leave, and then I was going to go find him again. I thought about it for a long time."

Ice water fills my stomach. "Oh? And...did you? Did you go and find him?" He'd better not say yes. I'm going to lose my fucking mind if he does. I especially asked him not to. I couldn't have made it any clearer—I didn't want the kid dead and dumped into the docks, regardless of what he may or may not have done.

Zeth lies down on the mattress, on his side, support-- ing himself on one elbow. He's leonine, all predator, thick muscles shifting and twisting as he uses his body in the most perplexing ways. No one else moves like he does. "I didn't go, no. I knew you'd fucking castrate me."

"Good. Because I would have. I'd have kicked your ass so hard, you wouldn't have been able to sit down for a year."

He looks impressed. "Only a year?"

"A decade. I never would have spoken to you again."

A slow, nefarious smirk spreads like honey across that perfect face of his. "I love that you think you could take me, angry girl. It turns me on to think of you trying to kick my ass."

"It shouldn't. It should instill fear and panic into you,

the likes of which you've never felt before."

Zeth is the owner of a multitude of barely visible tics that I've learned to decipher since I've been with him. Few others would be able to predict when he's going to strike, or when he's going to smile, but I can. I know he's trying not to laugh as we joust back and forth.

"I'm glad you didn't go back on your word," I tell him.

"I am, too."

"Promise me you're not going to? Promise me you won't do anything reckless?"

"I don't make promises like that, angry girl."

I would have known he was lying if he promised not to do anything reckless. It's physically *impossible* for him to avoid reckless. It should probably be his middle name or something: Zeth *Reckless* Mayfair. "All right. Then just promise me you won't keep anything from me again. We're a team. We're supposed to be in this together."

He looks unhappy about it, but he jerks his head once in a downward motion—as good as an oath in blood when it comes to my man.

"And promise you're not going to kill Mason in the next few weeks. That little girl needs her brother."

"You know what *I* need?" Zeth shunts himself closer to me, closing the gap between our bodies on the bed. "I need about ninety minutes with you, naked, here in this bed. And I need it *now*."

"Ninety minutes? That's a very long time. How do you plan to allocate all of these minutes?" I laugh as he

98

relieves me of my coffee cup and sets it back down on the bedside table. My smile is slipping as he leans into me, forcing me back onto the pillow. The mirth in his eyes is still there, but there's an edge to it now. A casual, secret enjoyment that tells me he knows perfectly well what he's going to do and he's going to enjoy it greatly.

"The first ten minutes are going to be me removing your clothes, angry girl. I'm going to torture you as I slip you out of these ridiculous pineapple print pajamas." He inches his face closer to mine, his eyebrows furrowing ever so slightly. I have to battle with myself not to fasten my teeth over that full bottom lip of his. Goddamn, he's so sexy. "Pineapples, Sloane? You trying to tell me something?"

My cheeks flush, heat spreading across my face, my lips tingling. He's done some questionable things to me with a pineapple before. I distinctly remember being very sticky and punch-drunk from his attentions in the aftermath; whenever I smell the saccharine sweet smell of cut fruit in the cafeteria at work, I'm instantly wet, a thrill of adrenalin ricocheting around my network of capillaries and major arteries like a spark chasing down a fuse, heading doggedly toward an impossible and unbearable explosion.

The upper right hand corner of Zeth's mouth twitches. "I haven't factored hitting the store for supplies into my ninety minute plan, I'm afraid," he tells me. "You're just going to have to make do with my fingers. My tongue. My cock. Promise me you're not going to be too disappointed."

I sound like a flustered teenager when I laugh, way too breathy and ruffled given how many times we've already fucked, but he does this to me. When he pins me down with that look of seduction in his eyes, I fall into him like light falling into a black hole, unable to deny the gravity that pulls me closer. It's physics, after all. Physics and chemistry. I can't fight the laws of the universe, and I sure as hell can't fight the lust that burns inside me like napalm.

There are people out there that believe in the law of attraction. Each morning they wake up and stand in front of a mirror, staring at their reflections, telling themselves that today money will enter into their lives. They'll get that job promotion. Their lives will be better and more satisfying in whatever way they desire. I don't need any of that. I don't need money. I don't need a better job, or a new car, or to travel the world. If I were to stand in front of a mirror and plead with the universe for anything, it would be this man, inside me, twenty-four fucking seven, his hands on my breasts and his mouth on my clit. I'm so abruptly turned on that I don't know what to do with myself, as Zeth pops up onto his knees so he can hover his body over mine, his dark eyes studious picking me apart with the precision of a heart surgeon.

"After the clothes are off, I'm going to spend the next

fifteen minutes licking and kissing your body. I want a lesson in anatomy, Dr. Romera. I want to know the medical term for each and every point where my tongue meets your skin."

"I'm not sure my brain works under that kind of pressure."

"It had better. Or there will be dire, *dire* consequences." Moving swiftly, he ducks, biting down hard and unexpectedly on my collarbone; I gasp, warring between my need to reel away from the pain and lean into it at the same time. Zeth chuckles in a dark, merciless way.

"Then I'm going to go down on you," Zeth informs me. "I'm going to feast on that pussy of yours. I'm going to stroke my tongue up and down you. I'm going to tease it inside of you. I'm going to eat your ass until you beg me to stop."

I buck underneath him, trying to squirm away. "No, you're not!"

He grabs hold of me, pinning me by my wrists to the bed. "What? You don't want me to eat your ass?"

"*No!*" Jesus. As if he needs to ask that. It's one thing feeling his fingers there, his hard cock, but his tongue? That just seems very wrong. Especially since my job is heavily focused on hygiene and keeping things clean.

Zeth's laughter grows louder. Somehow, even more wicked. "Oh dear, angry girl. I thought I'd already shocked the prude right out of you. Seems I was wrong."

"You're not going anywhere near my ass with your mouth."

"Maybe you're the one that needs the lesson in anatomy. Hate to tell you this, doc, but your pussy is very close to your ass. I've spent a considerable amount of time down there already, and let me tell you…I've never had more fun in my entire life."

I squirm some more, only half-heartedly trying to get free. "My ass is not to be licked!"

"Every time you protest, I'm allocating another three minutes to that area of your body," he informs me. His expression is serious, the tone of his voice deep and resonant. He's not laughing anymore, which tells me I better shut the fuck up or he's going to be making me writhe against his mouth for a full half an hour. He's not really going to do it, though. He wouldn't, surely?

"That should take us up to forty minutes," he says evenly. "The next fifteen minutes are for me. Can you guess what I'm going to make you do, angry girl? Do you think you know what I want from you?"

Never in my life have I been the kind of person to bite my lip. Every time I see a woman do it in the movies, it makes me want to smash my fist through the damn screen and scream at the chick to grow some backbone. But right now? If I were a lip biter, right now I'd be damn near trying to chew the thing clean off. I shake my head, a little too intimidated to speak.

Zeth pouts in a way that makes the hairs on the back

of my neck stand to attention. "Well," he says. "I'm going to want you on the bed, Sloane. On your back. Your head will be hanging off the edge, and I'm going to stand over you. You're going to open your mouth for me." He frees one of his hands, gripping both my wrists with ease in just his right, so he can trace his fingertips lightly over my lips. He pushes his index finger between them, forcing my mouth open. His finger probes inside, running over teeth and tongue. He pushes my mouth open wider, humming to himself, eyes fixed on what he's doing. He looks fascinated, like he's already imagining enacting his plans and how good it's going to feel.

"I'm going to slide myself in there, angry girl. I'm going to fuck your mouth until you can't take it anymore. You're going to feel me sliding all the way down, deep into your throat, and you're going to love it."

I press my legs together, the muscles in my thighs locking up tight. It feels wrong to admit that I believe him, I *am* going to love it, but I know that I will. His hands in my hair, pulling tighter and tighter as he grows so hard in my mouth; the way his legs lock when he skirts close to coming; the way his breath becomes ragged and intense—all of these things drive me crazy when I go down on him. And when he's a little rough...god, I don't know what the hell is wrong with me. I am so ready to jump him and do this already. I want him. No, I *need* him.

My desire to climb him like a tree is fierce. I want to

take hold of the hem of his t-shirt, to bunch it up in my hands, to rip it off over his head, but Zeth still has hold of me by the wrists. They're pinned high over my head, far from the smooth, solid, delicious feel of his skin, and that is almost too much to bear.

"Would you like me to come in your mouth?" he whispers. "When my cock is deep in your throat, do you want to feel me getting closer and closer? Do you want to hear me roar when I explode everywhere, so you can taste me on your tongue?" He asks me so intensely, brows still knotted together, unblinking, that he looks severe. His mouth is only two inches away from mine. I can't stop staring at his lips.

Sweet Jesus. I'm a lost cause. I'm done for. I'll never be the same again. "Yes," I tell him. "I want you to come in my mouth. Please, Zeth. *Please*."

"Good girl. You're a very good girl."

I am *his* good girl. Ever since I was old enough to think about such things, I've made a conscious effort never to measure myself by what other people think of me, particularly if their approval has been on the line. I've never wanted it. I've never needed it. Not even with my parents. I've always wanted to make *myself* proud, to work hard *for me*, to accomplish my best *for me*. But this man...shit, I don't even know where to begin when I try to analyze how he makes me feel. It brings me such intense, unfathomable pleasure to make him happy. When he tells me that he's pleased with me, I'm filled with such a pride that it almost makes me embarrassed. I live for it, though. I crave it like a drug. I wouldn't sacrifice it for the world.

Zeth withdraws his fingers from my mouth, rubbing the pad of his index finger against the swell of my lip. He groans in the most electrifying way, and then he says, "Still plenty of time left. I'm going to give you what you want. I'm going to come in your mouth, but I'm still going to be hard for you. Once I'm done there, we're still going to have another thirty-five minutes. Do you know what I'm going to do then, Sloane?"

"What?" He isn't going to have to touch me to make me come at this rate. My nipples are peaked to painful degrees; every time I shift underneath him, they rub against the light material of my pineapple covered shirt, sending shockwave after shockwave of longing through me, making me pant.

"Then," he says, lowering himself the tiniest bit further, baring his teeth a little. It's such an animalistic, raw thing to do that my toes curl. "*Then*, I'm going to fuck you long, and I'm going to fuck you hard. I'm going to make you scream my name so goddamn loud that your neighbors three miles away are going to know who I am, and they're gonna high five me in the mother-fucking street. I'm going to bring you so close to coming that you're delirious with need, and then I'm going to stop, over and over again, until all I need to do is blow on your skin to make you explode. Do you think you can take it?"

"Yes. Fuck, Zeth. Yes."

"And are you ready?"

I nod, swallowing. My throat feels dry. My body is vibrating with a mixture of nerves and anticipation. Zeth sits back on his heels, observing me with a calmness that makes my heart trip over itself in the most terrifying way.

"Good," he says. "Then let's begin."

Mason

five days later

"I want to take her home. She's bored out of her mind down here. She's been fine for days now. It's *time*." I lean against the wall by the elevator, pleading my case to Sloane. No, the extra treatment Millie's receiving isn't costing anything, and yes, I sure as hell am grateful, but fuck! I want to disentangle myself from Zeth & his girlfriend (wouldn't *that* have been valuable information to know) as much as I can. I owe Sloane my life; I already owed her way more than that before, when she helped with Millie. No one else would have stepped up for my sister the way she did. I can't bear the thought of owing her any more.

"What's the harm in keeping her in another couple of days?" she asks. Seeing her here is very different to seeing her outside of the hospital walls. Here, she's the epitome of calm and efficiency, almost to the point where she appears mechanical. Like nothing at all fazes her. When I saw her at Zeth's warehouse, she had been flustered and fiery. It's hard to imagine her like that, now, as she flips through Millie's chart. "Her sleep pattern's irregular. She's complaining of stomachache a couple of times a day. Both of those things could be underlying symptoms for something more serious."

"She's being left alone in an unfamiliar place every night. She can't sleep because she needs her own bed. And she's got stomachache half the time because Dr. Bochowitz keeps giving her all the chocolate pudding she can eat instead of her regular meals."

"Seriously?"

I shove away from the wall, following after her as she begins to walk off down the corridor. "*Seriously*. Trust me, okay. Millie's going to be ten times better off at home, back to her normal routine, than she is here. I'm grateful for everything you've done, but it's *enough*."

Romera stops walking. "Okay. Take her home. But you call me the moment you think she looks under the weather, you hear me? Day or night. It doesn't matter." She hands me a business card, the kind all doctors have, a string of unintelligible letters tacked together at the end of their names. I pocket it, smiling. "Thanks, Doc. I will, I promise."

"Good. I need to clear morning rounds. It's a miracle

you even caught me this early. I don't need to see you out, do I?"

I shake my head.

"Then I guess I'll be seeing you. Hopefully not too soon."

"Hey, Dr. Romera?"

She hooks the tubing of a stethoscope over her neck. "Yes?"

"It said on that card of yours that you're a trauma surgeon. That true?"

She nods. "Why do you ask?"

"You were in business clothes before, but now you're in scrubs. I thought you might have been banned from operating or something."

She clasps hold of both ends of the stethoscope, fingers wrapped around the instrument like it's her most prized possession. "Something like that," she says. "I had the flu. You're not allowed into the OR if you're contagious, Mr. Reeves. I'm sure I'll be cleared for surgery any day, though."

••••

Wanda's so pleased to see Millie at her front door that she refuses to accept the crumpled ten-dollar bill I try to offer her. "I done told you once, I told you a thousand times, boy. That girl is welcome here any time. If I'm home, she can come play with Brandy anytime she likes."

"I know, I know," I tell her. "It'll be late by the time I get back, though." I feel super shitty; after fighting so hard to take Millie home, I should be spending the night in with her, but I need to work. I need to make money.

Wanda shakes her head, closing my fist around the money I'm still holding out to her. "It's not a problem, Mason. I got her, don't you worry. I'll make sure I feed her and give her a bath. Now hurry on out of here before you're late. It's already after eight."

"Ssshhhh—" I manage to stop myself before I curse. Wanda isn't a fan of curse words. After eight, though? I got up at five am to go find Romera at the hospital. How can it be so late now? Wanda hooks a perfectly plucked eyebrow, giving me a warning glance. "Sorry. Hurrying's not going to save me now, though. I'm already late," I tell her.

"Well, then get on with you!"

I kiss Millie on top of the head, brushing down the fine strands of her hair as she grins up at me. "I'll see you later, mouse. Be good for Miss Wanda, okay?"

She's never anything but good, yet Millie nods her head dutifully. She doesn't go into Wanda's place until I'm down the hall and gone from sight.

I've got a lead foot and I'm blind to the color red as I burn across town. Mac's in his office when I pull up outside the garage. He's on the phone, shouting at someone as I hurry across the forecourt and stick my head under the hood of the Chevy Impala I've been working on restoring the past couple of days. I think I've gotten away with being close to twenty minutes late, but then Mac sticks his head around his office door and hollers at the top of his lungs.

"Get your ass in here, fuckhead! *Move!*"

Shit.

I'm always surprised by how tidy Mac's office is. By the look of him, stained vest, ripped pants, grease everywhere—the auto mechanic's universal uniform— you'd think he'd be messy in all aspects of his life. Turns out he's pretty OCD, though. Not a paper is out of place on his desk. Almanacs and mechanics guides relating to a vast array of car manufactures are neatly arranged by year and by size on the shelves behind him. The waste paper bin beside his dark stained wooden desk is empty. No pin up girls on the walls. No food wrappers, or empty soda cans. It's neat as a pin.

"You think I'm a fucking joke, don't you?" Mac spits. By the wiry vein pulsing in the center of his forehead, and the cloudy bead of sweat running down the side of his face, I can see today was a bad day to be late.

"Absolutely not. Of course I don't."

"Then why in *fuck* would you think it's okay to show up to work late? AGAIN?"

"I'm sorry. I was at the hospital. Fuck, Mac, I'm trying my be—"

He holds up one hand. "Don't even think about finishing that sentence. I know your kid sister is sick. I know you got a lot on your plate, Mason, I do, but so does every other fucker on the face of the planet. I'm trying to run a business here. Figure this shit out, or you're gonna be looking for another job. We clear?"

I want to punch a hole in the bastard's face. It would be more than satisfying to watch him crumple like the sack of shit he is as I plant a solid right hook straight into his skull, but where would that leave me? Without a steady income, and a blackened reputation. Mac is alpha and omega when it comes to body shop repairs in Seattle. One word from him and I'd never work in this city again.

"Yes, Mac. I got it. We're clear."

"All right then." His face softens a little. "And like I'm always saying, if these morning shifts are too tricky for you, you can always take up some night work. I'm never short of that."

As always, I turn him down flat. Mac's night work is the most illegal, dangerous, and generally life threatening under-the-table work you could hope to find. I need money, not a criminal record or a shallow grave. "Thanks for the offer, though." I turn and I get the hell out of there, before he can hint at anything else, and I can feel the sweat running down in between my shoulder blades. I'd better finish this car today, get her up and running in record time, remind Mac that I'm the best there is, otherwise I'm not going to be able to keep him off my back much longer.

I get to work, trying not to look in the direction of Mac's office, or at the gym across the road, where Zeth is no doubt training hard, thrashing the shit out of a sea of unsuspecting wanna be fighters.

Later, after lunch (which I work right through), a familiar, beaten up looking Hyundai pulls up on the street outside the garage, and I instantly know this means trouble. I fixed that car a few weeks ago. Not only that, but I had the pleasure of driving its owner to her class at Seattle University.

Kaya.

She climbs out of the car, pulling her coat tighter around her shoulders, jerking the fur-lined hood up over that pixie cut of hers. For a moment, I trick myself into thinking that she's not coming into the garage. Why the fuck would she? People don't just show up at other people's places of employment, wanting to have a chat. It just doesn't happen. But the way she slams the car door closed and makes a beeline right for me is unmistakable. I should know better than to think Kaya Rayne conforms to any form of social etiquette.

"Hey." The word forms on a cloud as her breath fogs the air. "You got a minute? I need to talk to you."

I look at her like she's crazy. "No, I don't have a minute. I'm at work. I—*fuck*, Kaya. Leave. *Please.* I'm in enough shit as it is already today."

A hurt look flashes across her cold-flushed face. "You really need to hear what I have to say, Mason. I'm not messing around."

"Neither am I. If my boss sees you here, talking to me, my ass is in the can."

"Don't be such a baby. Listen to m—"

"I'd love to listen to you. Standing around, shooting the shit with you while you tell me about your day sounds fucking spiffy, but if Mac catches me socializing while I'm on the clock, I might as well pack up my tools and take off right now. Can we do this later?"

Kaya, lost in her gigantic parka, frowns at me, and I already know the power of that frown. She probably uses that thing to get whatever she wants, whenever she wants. It's probably been used to bring men far more resilient than me to their knees.

"When?" she ask.

"I don't know. *Later.*"

"Tonight?"

"Fine. Yes, tonight. I finish at eight. I'll meet you at the café on the corner. Now, please. Just go!"

She goes.

ELEVEN

Sloane

You never get used to the smell of vomit, even when it's your own. I'm supposed to be attending a check up in thirty minutes so I can get signed off and back onto the OR floor, but there's no chance of that happening today. I've been puking my guts up since lunchtime, and it doesn't look like I'll be stopping any time soon. I grab the bottle of blue Gatorade in front of me and swig some, swirling it around my mouth before spitting it into the toilet.

Jesus. Talk about stomach bug.

I'm shaky on my feet as I make my way off the emergency room floor and up to the ICU. That's where I run into Oliver. He smiles when he sees me. In fact, he grins from ear to ear. The grin fades when he gets a good look at me, though. "Goddamn, Romera, you look like death warmed up. What the hell's the matter with you?"

I chug the Gatorade, wiping my mouth with the back of my hand. "Still sick," I say, pulling a face.

"Then you probably shouldn't be here," he says.

"Screw you. I'm already off surgery. You can't send me home altogether. I'll go mad."

"You stay here and you're gonna infect half the people you see in the emergency room. That's all I'm saying."

I know he's right, but damn. I really don't want to be quarantined at the house. I'm no good at being ill. I don't know the meaning of bed rest. I'll end up gutting the kitchen, spring-cleaning like a crazy woman, or back burning all the dead shrubs and deadfall at the rear of the house. I'll probably end up starting a forest fire. "Don't you dare report me, Oliver Massey," I say. "I'll never forgive you. I swear I'll take it easy. I'll do paperwork upstairs or something. I promise I won't infect anyone."

He looks doubtful. "All right. But you're submitting to an IV before you go anywhere, okay? You look like dog shit."

"Gee. Thanks."

He takes me by the arm and drags me into an examination room, pulling on a pair of rubber gloves with way too much flourish. He's enjoying this. With a ridiculous waggle of his eyebrows, he pushes down on my shoulders, forcing me to take a seat on the edge of the gurney behind me. "Now. Dr. Romera. Do you happen to have a severe case of explosive diarrhea?"

"Gross. No."

"Hmm." He's disappointed, I can tell. "That's strange. Everyone else has had it. Myself included. Really humiliating when you're sleeping at your new girlfriend's house."

"Oh *no*."

"Oh *yeah*." He holds the back of his hand against my forehead, checking my temperature.

"We have far more accurate ways of doing that, you know?"

"I'm too lazy to grab a thermometer. Besides, you don't have a fever. You're fine."

"Yeah, I don't feel hot."

Oliver scrutinizes my face, looking me over, as if merely staring at me will provide him with a diagnosis. "Well, I guess you're on the other end of it, then," he says. "Some fluids aren't going to hurt, either way."

I lay back on the gurney, propped up with pillows, the backrest in an upright position, and Oliver goes about hooking me up to the IV beside the bed. He pokes his tongue out at me, then proceeds to ask me the things we're meant to ask every time we administer any kind of treatment to a patient:

"Are you allergic to anything?"

"No."

"On any medications right now?"

"No."

"Had any recent surgeries?"

"No."

"Any history of heart problems?"

"No."

"Any chance you might be pregnant?"

"No."

"When was your last period?"

I'm about to reel off the information, but that isn't one of the standard questions. I shoot daggers at Oliver. He tries to distract me by sliding the IV needle into my skin, but it doesn't work. "I'm not pregnant, Oliver. I'm on birth control. Now hurry the hell up. This is already going to take up half my afternoon."

He shrugs his shoulders, turning down the corners of his mouth. "Just being thorough, Romera. I know you. You're busy, you forget to take the pill a couple of times in a row, and BAM! Knocked up. I've seen that dude you're living with, you forget. He looks like he has strong swimmers."

"Stop talking about Zeth's swimmers. His swimmers are none of your business. And I'm on the injection, so you don't need to fret. No chance I can forget if I need to go get a needle jabbed into my ass cheek every three months, now, is there?"

"Fair enough." Oliver holds up his hands in surrender. "Just lookin' out for you," he says, laughing.

"Why are you so cheery, anyway?" I grumble. I don't

need to mention the last time I saw him, when he was frustrated to the point of anger in the resident's locker room.

"I am cheery because Alex is being moved down from the ICU today. He's finally in the clear," he says. "Providing no secondary infections have been festering away in the background, it's just a matter of recuperation and physio now."

"Damn, Oliver, I'm so relieved to hear that. I'm so happy for you."

"Yeah, me too. Thanks, Romera. And thanks for being the one to help me stitch him back together in the first place. Now get better already so we can fix some more people, huh?"

I give him a mock salute. "Sir, yes, sir."

"The guys from Alex's fire house are coming by later. They haven't been able to see him properly until now. I think they mentioned something about beer and Philly cheesesteak sandwiches if you think you might be able to stomach it."

"You underestimate me. I can always stomach a Philly cheesesteak."

Oliver leaves me to my own devices as I sit there, letting the IV do it's work. It's tedious, just letting time pass, and I have nothing to do but let my mind wander.

Zeth's probably training hard, dreaming of ways to quash the threat Lowell poses once and for all. Hopefully without killing anyone. Michael's probably...I have no idea what Michael's probably doing. If he's not with Zeth, then his actions or his whereabouts are a mystery. He's such a guarded guy. His personal life is so unknown to me that I don't even have a clue if he's single or not. I doubt he has time for a girlfriend, considering how much time he spends running errands or 'fixing things' for Zeth, but there is a slim chance he's got someone tucked away somewhere. I hope he has.

I think about Alex Massey, then. I think about how lucky he is that he'll be walking out of St. Peter's in a couple of week's time. It could so easily have gone another way. The surgery could have killed him. Infection could have spread, bacteria overtaking him from the inside out. He was on any number of seriously strong, seriously dangerous anti-virals and painkillers. They could have interacted, as they sometimes do depending on the person, either sending him floating off into the ether or rendering the antivirals ineffective. There were so many things that could have gone wrong. So many things that could have…

Oh god.

I suddenly feel very, very sick again. My stomach rolls, nausea washing over me, as the room tilts uncomfortably. It's not just the return of the nausea that's making me feel ill. It's the horrific, terrifying realization that just hit me like a bowling ball to the head. Alex was on a multitude of conflicting meds. Meds that could have made him even worse than he already was. Meds that could have caused others to fail and not work. *I* recently took meds that could cause others to fail and not work. I—shit, how could I have been so stupid? How could I have not thought for one second?

The antibiotics I took when I first got sick...antibiotics that occasionally render all forms of birth control utterly, completely, frighteningly ineffective.

••••

Ward seven wasn't built to accommodate twelve drunk fire fighters, and yet somehow Oliver has managed to squeeze them in. Alex Massey's a special case, but he's not special enough to warrant an entire ward all to himself. He's rooming with a ninety-four-year old woman, who's recovering from a triple bypass. Far from being upset about the ruckus, Cynthia May Allerdyce, hard of hearing and prone to bouts of obnoxious farting, is thoroughly enjoying the show the fire fighters are putting on for her. The guys, at least three or four beers in, could easily have been extras in Magic Mike, and they all know it. They're enjoying themselves way too much as each of them lets Cynthia rub up on their chests and their abs with her arthritic hands. A couple of the guys aren't even that built, some of them are kind of rotund around the mid-section, and yet they're the worst offenders. Poor Cynthia is flushed in the face as she chats with the smoke chasers, patting them on the shoulders and telling them what good boys they are.

Alex Massey sits up in bed, watching with amusement as his friends make fools of themselves. No Philly cheesesteak for Alex. No beer, either. Just good ol' morphine. Oliver hovers close to his brother, talking, constantly checking to see if he's feeling all right. When he sees me on the other side of the bay, surreptitiously watching Cynthia's monitor to see if she's about to go into cardiac arrest, he gives me a grin and a small wave.

"Is he your boyfriend, sweetie?" Cynthia's hand is cold on my arm, her skin like ice. She may be coming upon ninety-five, but she has the clear, intelligent eyes of a nineteen-year-old. She wears the look of someone who's lived a life. Who knows what amazing stories she has to share. I'd love to sit down with her and hear them all, but that would be impossible with all the cheering and laughter that currently fills the room.

"Him? Dr. Massey? No." I shake my head. "He's a very good friend of mine, though."

"Shame. He's a good looking, tall drink of water, no?" She has the most charming soft southern twang. I bet she was quite the southern belle back in her day. I squeeze her hand.

"I already have a boyfriend, Cynthia."

"Is he as good lookin' as him?" she says the words like she already can't believe that it's true.

"He sure is. He's the hottest man to ever walk the surface of the earth."

"Aww, honey." She says the word *honeh*, instead of honey. "You might believe that, and good. Sometimes a man can be the most...*hideous* thang, and still some woman out there love him warts an' all. I do believe you one of those women, capable a' lovin' somethin' no one else could."

I laugh, patting her hand. Her skin feels so thin, like a moth's wing. "My boyfriend's handsome, believe me. Still, I guess you're right. Some people might have trouble finding it in themselves to love him."

"Mmm-hmm. Well you tell him from me, I know a kahhhnd soul when I see one, and he got hisself the kindest there is. I hope he takes good care of you, child."

"He does," I tell her, saying it with conviction, because it's the truth, after all. Zeth takes the best care of me. "He's a good man."

Cynthia nods, her attention drawn away by the fire fighters, and I find myself numbed by my last statement. *He's a good man.*

Is Zeth a good man? I love him without question; I care for him beyond measure, but is he a *good* man? My head's experience of the past year tells me one thing, the evidence on paper showing a stark, unfriendly reality, but my heart reports an altogether different experience. I try not to think about the unsettling thought that came to me while I was letting that IV do its work. I'm just being stupid, I'm sure. I'm probably wrong. There's no way I can be pregnant. No fucking way. There's one way to be sure, of course: I could go do a test. But for some reason I can't seem to make myself do it. If I pee on a stick, if I do a blood test just to be sure, that means I may have to face an unpleasant truth, and I don't think I can bear that right now. Scratch that—I *know* I can't.

Oliver and Alex both smile at me as I hover close to them. They both have the same shaped eyes, the same shaped faces, the same honey blond hair that curls up a little around their ears. When they're apart, I'd never say either one of them looks too much like the other, their mannerisms making them seem unrelated altogether, and yet sit them side-by-side and you wonder how you ever doubted their blood ties.

"Don't worry. I'm not gonna give you a hug," I tell Alex. "I don't want to get you sick. Just wanted to come say hello. I'm so glad you're on the mend." Could be that I wouldn't get him sick—unlike the flu, pregnancy isn't catching, after all—but it's not worth the risk.

Alex waves me off, like his life wasn't in any real danger to begin with. "Can't wait to get back to work," he says. "These four walls are starting to drive me nuts already. And these assholes won't quit calling me lazy, either. I need to get back on the rig, show them how it's done."

"If getting crushed and almost dying is how you do it, we don't wanna know," a young guy with a buzzed head says, laughing.

"Whatever, man. You're just jealous that I get to hang

out with hot doctors all day long."

The kid with the buzz cut rolls his eyes. "You think I struggle getting tail? Do you? Really? I bet if I asked this lovely young thing out on a date, she'd say yes, wouldn't you, doc?" He sends a heavily suggestive wink my way.

"Don't you be hassling that young woman," Cynthia calls. "She's got a beau at home already. Why don't you come and lay some of that charm on this single old woman, huh? I wouldn't mind the attention none." The cheeky old girl has a goddamn beer bottle in her hand. I grab it from her just before she can raise it to her lips and take a swig.

"Whoa, now. You aren't allowed that, Miss Cynthia. You just had heart surgery."

"What about intercourse?" she asks. "You know… *nookie*. Might that be possible?" She cuts her eyes at the fire fighter standing next to her, her eyes glinting brightly. He pretends like he didn't hear her, but the tips of his ears are turning redder and redder by the second, and I can't help but feel a little sorry for the guy; she's incorrigible.

"I'm afraid you need to lay off any strenuous physical activity for the next little while as well. Your doctor will give you the go-ahead when he thinks you're fit enough to cope with the…*excitement*."

Cynthia beams at the fire fighter. "Think you could come back and visit in a few weeks, hot stuff?"

125

TWELVE

Zeth

The thing about promises is that they're often really inconvenient and difficult to keep. I swore I wouldn't put Mason in the ground for what he's done, but I wonder just how pissed Sloane will be if I just gave him a gentle beating? A light ass kicking? Just one little black eye? Seems unfair to me that I should be expected to leave him entirely in one piece. Really, if there was any justice in the world, I'd be allowed to give him a good hiding just once.

Now all I'm allowed to do is use him to feed information to Lowell, and that's nowhere near as satisfying. Could come in handy, though. It's been five days and I haven't come up with something appropriate to have him relay yet, but I'm sure I'll think of something. In the meantime, I have to make sure everything appears normal. The gym has to be opened. Sloane has to go to work. Mason still has to come train after he's done at the auto mechanics—which I personally fucking hate, I don't even want to lay eyes on the fucker—and Michael has to keep doing his thing, too.

So there it is. Business as usual.

I'm driving across the city toward the gym when I notice the Denali with tinted windows behind me, following two cars back. *That* certainly isn't business as usual. I drive this route every day, twice a day, sometimes more, and I'm always hyper aware of my surroundings. No way a Denali would be tailing me for so long, indicating, changing lanes, taking exits exactly as I take exits, without there being some reason. That reason is obvious: Lowell's gotten bored of waiting for me to slip up and do something wrong, so she's following me, waiting for the right moment to pounce. It's a surprise she hasn't arrested me already, given her propensity to act first and figure shit out later, but maybe her higher ups have slapped her wrists a couple of times. Her partner was killed months back at a shoot out in the fucking hospital, for crying out loud. It's a miracle she's allowed anywhere near this case.

I downshift, slowing so I can drift casually into the right hand lane. Up ahead, the turn off for Hunt's Point is fast approaching. I indicate, steering the car onto the exit ramp, watching in the rear view mirror as, two cars back, the Denali with the blackened out windows follows my lead. Only one car between us now. My brain switches to autopilot, following an automatic route through quiet, leafy neighborhood streets, past oversized McMansions, Mexican gardeners with woolen hats pulled down low over their ears, kids in strollers, dogs on leads, and the Denali follows.

She has to fucking know I've made her by now. No way she can think I haven't noticed her, practically jammed up my exhaust pipe. She should be way fucking better at this. I quit looking in my rear view, and I'm shocked when I realize where I've driven myself. The old house I grew up in looms high above the road, set back in amongst a wall of eight-foot high pine and spruce trees. The corner of the basketball court out the back of the house is just about visible, as I roll the Camaro up alongside the curb. The hairs on the back of my neck are standing on end.

I never made a plan where I decided I would never come back to this house. A plan like that didn't seem necessary. Why the fuck would I come back to Charlie's place? To the place where I fought off demons in the night. To the place where nightmares were real, tangible, wicked things that would haunt you the moment you closed your eyes.

Behind me, the Denali comes to a halt as well. You have got to be fucking *kidding* me? This bitch is insane. Can she really have balls this big? She must want me to know she's following me; that's the only explanation for this blatant behavior. Well, if she thinks she's going to intimidate me, she has another fucking thing coming. Psycho bitch. I get out of the car, slamming the door closed behind me, and I storm up to the driver's window of the Denali, blood surging through my veins, head pounding, my body already charged and ready for violence. Will I hit her? Damn fucking right I will. I think about knocking on the window, waiting for it to buzz down before unleashing my fists, but I can't talk myself into being so polite. Instead, I pull back my hand and I swing, smashing my way through the thickened glass. Car windows are designed to shatter, and the Denali's window does exactly that, the glass exploding into a thousand tiny cubed pieces and raining down on the sidewalk. Inside, I hear someone scrambling, rearing back as the glass pours in on them, too.

"Fuck! Fuck you, man!" someone yells. A guy? So Lowell had one of her lackeys in the driver's seat. Why am I not surprised? I can picture her in the back seat of the car, barking out orders as her little DEA minion obeys her every command. I'm just waiting for the bitch to climb out of the car, cool as cool can be, ready to threaten arrest for damage to government property, when the polished, unmistakable barrel of a gun appears through the broken window.

"Back up, motherfucker. Back the fuck up *right now*."

DEA agents can't just fucking shoot you for no reason, but then again I have given them a reason. I'm a hostile; I just attacked their car. It would be so fucking easy for them to get away with plugging me full of bullets and letting me bleed out right here on the cement.

I hate to have to give this guy what he wants, but I also don't feel like getting shot in the face today. I take a step back from the window. Where the fuck is my gun? How in god's name did I climb out of the Camaro without the fucking thing? I guess if I get shot and die right now, it'll serve me fucking right. More glass tinkles onto the sidewalk as the driver tries to open his door, which seems to be jammed. A long moment follows, where the idiot inside the vehicle throws some weight behind the door and eventually forces it open. He climbs out of the car, still holding the gun in one hand, while brushing fragments of glass from his lap with the other.

Suit and tie. Not a DEA suit and tie—no, it's way too nice to have been purchased on a civil servant's pay check. Looks like Armani. Michael would know better than me, but he's not here to confirm either way. Dark shades. Slicked back hair. The kind of stubble guys pay forty dollars in a barber's shop to have shaped and kept neat and tidy while they sip on a complimentary beer. I find myself suddenly doubtful. This guy's a cop? No fucking way. He oozes attitude, which wouldn't have necessarily ruled him out as five-oh, but there's something else…

The way he's holding his gun.

Cops all hold their guns the same way, shoulder

hitched up, elbow locked and rigid, left hand cupped underneath the right, providing a stable platform of support. They stare at you down the length of their weapons, locking you in their sights, ready at all times to pull the trigger and end your life. It's a recognizable stance, the country over, and this guy doesn't have it.

He holds his gun like a criminal, like he's pointing a finger at you and the weapon is merely an extension of his hand. He's not aiming the thing. He's just stabbing it in my general direction, expecting it to do all of the hard work on its own. "You just made a big fucking mistake, Mr. Mayfair," he tells me. "This is an airport rental, and I didn't get insurance."

"More fool you," I grind out through clenched teeth. "Should have known better if you planned on following a guy like me around like a bad fucking smell. Where the hell is she?"

"*She?*" The dark-haired guy frowns as he removes the safety from his handgun. "I'm afraid you've lost me."

"*Lowell.*" It's worth a shot. If I see one flicker of recognition on the guy, I'll know he's acting with Denise.

"I don't know any Lowell, Mr. Mayfair. The only woman I know in town is that hot piece of ass girlfriend of yours. What's she called again? Sarah? No, that's it. *Sloane.*"

I say nothing. I don't want to lose my cool too soon. If he mentions Sloane one more time, I won't be able to help myself, but in the meantime I need to figure out what the fuck is going on. "Why the *fuck* are you following me?" I snarl.

The guy shrugs, the hand that's holding his gun wavering as he makes a disinterested pout. "Just doing what I'm told, I'm afraid. I've come a long way to see you, Mr. Mayfair."

"I'm a very busy man. You should have made an appointment."

"I would have, but I don't like your secretary too much. A little too...*masculine* for my liking. I prefer them to be a little leggier. Big boobs. No predisposition to murder anyone who happens to show up on their doorstep without an invitation."

"What can I say? Michael knows who I have time for and who I don't. He's very good at his job."

"And *I* am good at mine."

I detect the clipped cadence of his speech and the hint of an accent—a Bronx or Brooklyn twang that tells me this guy isn't from here. At best guess, he's a New Yorker. He's a little far from home if that's the case. I smile, the right side of my mouth twisting upward as I scan him for further details that might tell me exactly where he's come from and what his plans are here. He must want violence. No one in their right minds would track me down and take me on if they just wanted to hang out. The guy brushes back his hair, flattening down the section that's escaped the oil slick product he has in there, and is hanging down into his face.

"Gonna introduce yourself?" I ask.

"My name's Milo Barbieri. I doubt you've heard of me." He says this like it's a joke, though, and I obviously must know exactly who he is. I've heard the last name, of course, but Milo? He's not one of Roberto's sons. Not even a nephew. He must be a distant relative or something. Someone low ranking enough that they've had to make the trip across the county to see little ol' me. I'm fucking flattered.

"You hide behind those shades all day?" I snap. I want to get a proper look at this asshole.

"Only when the sun's out," he replies. "Don't worry. If you're wondering what kind of guy I am, I can give you a brief rundown and we can dispense with the posturing. I'm one of the bad guys. I steal money from old ladies. I've killed a bunch of people. I've been in jail more times than I can count. What about you, Mr. Mayfair? You're the same as me, no?"

"Maybe once upon a time. Not anymore."

The guy with the gun looks a little saddened. "So the legends of the infamous Zeth Mayfair are all untrue. I have to say, that's a little disappointing. I thought I might get to have a little fun with you while I was out here. Thought maybe we could tear it up, raise some hell. I can see I was wrong."

This guy is testing my patience. He's incompetent as fuck—I could rush him and take that weapon from him any second and he wouldn't see me coming. Some men think they're in charge because they're holding a weapon, the same way some men think they get to fuck because they have their dicks in their hands. They don't seem to realize that without pulling the trigger, in both situations their posturing is nothing more than masturbation. "Just get on with it," I growl. "Why the fuck are you here?" I already know he's organized crime. Disorganized crime, more like. I just need to hear him say it.

"My boss sent me to see if you've had time to reconsider his offer, Mr. Mayfair," he informs me.

"And your boss would be the Butcher, of course?"

"Correct. He called you personally not too long ago, offering to form an allegiance with you. You were very rude to him, Mr. Mayfair. Very rude indeed."

"Apologies," I say, my voice thick with sarcasm. "But as you can imagine, I don't like being threatened."

"Mr. Barbieri didn't threaten you, Zeth. He merely asked you to join forces with him. He offered you quite a sweet deal, if I recall correctly. All of Seattle in return for your obedience. That's more than he's ever offered anyone else."

"And if I refused to offer him my obedience, I would be seen as a danger to his operation. If that's not a threat, then I don't know what is."

"You're mistaken. That was simply…" He shrugs. "A display of logic? You're a well-respected man, Zeth. People in this town won't fuck with you. If you say something is law, the people selling drugs, guns and women in this town accept that it's fucking law. If you say the Italians aren't allowed to expand their business to the west coast, then people are going to rebel against it. They'll get ideas about how they can and can't interact with us. My employer, Mr. Barbieri, he doesn't like friction, see. He's a man that likes things to run smoothly at all times. No dissention. No civil wars or insurgency. He used to be in the military back in Italy, once upon a time, and he's retained that military mindset all his life. You can imagine how something messy and unfinished might make him uneasy. And this situation with you is definitely both messy and unfinished."

"I don't see it as either of those things," I tell him. "I think it's very clear cut. I'm not working for some psychotic bastard in New York. I'm not going to align myself with someone like him. My last boss was unhinged, and I'm sure yours is, too."

The guy makes a noncommittal grunting sound. "All men who lead are just a little crazy."

"Yes. And those who follow are even crazier. I'm done being a follower."

Leaning against the side of the car, the Italian takes a pack of cigarettes out of his pocket, removes one and places it between his lips. His polished silver lighter makes a loud *schink*-ing sound as he strikes the wheel against the leg of his pants. The flame flickers, almost guttering out before the cigarette is lit. "So, I go back to

New York, and I tell Mr. Barbieri what? That I came all the way out here and you turned me down flat? That ain't gonna fly, big man. It's one thing being rude to my boss on the phone. Being rude to an envoy? That's gonna piss him off beyond all belief."

"Damn. Now I feel bad. How pissed off is he gonna be when he sees what I've done to your face?"

The Italian draws on his cigarette. Blows out the smoke as he laughs. He scratches his temple with the slide of his gun. "You're a ridiculous human being, Mr. Mayfair. You've got balls. I don't get to meet many guys like you in my line of work. Hard men on the east coast...well, they're only hard until you point something sharp and shiny at them. After that, they're pissin' all over themselves and trying to sell their own mother in order to find their way into your good graces. You, on the other hand...I like you. You're not the kind of guy to back down from a fight, even when you know you can't win."

"Who says I can't win?"

The Italian holds up the gun in his hand, head angled to one side—*forgot about this, did you, jackhole?* He favors me with another one of those friendly, aren't-we-having-the-best-time bouts of airy laughter. "I heard some pretty intense things about you, man, but I've never heard anyone claim you're superman. Ain't no outrunning a bullet, Zeth."

"It's not a question of outrunning anything," I say.

"More a matter of aim. And focus. And nerve." I take a step toward him, ignoring the gun he has outstretched in his hand once more. The Italian takes another drag from his cigarette, blowing the fumes down his nose in twin plumes of smoke cloud around his head.

"I don't miss, Zeth. If you want to find that out for yourself, be my guest."

I do want to find out for myself. To be fair to this guy, whoever the fuck he is, he has some balls himself. We're out in the open in the middle of the day, in a neighborhood not known for it's high crime rate. He's standing here like he hasn't got a care in the world, waving a gun around like it's his rolled up morning newspaper. I don't doubt for a second that he will shoot. I don't doubt for a second that he's a good shot; the familiarity and ease with which he holds his weapon says he's spent a lot of quality bonding time with it. I do think he has underestimated me, though. See, I'm a big fucking guy. I'm tall and I'm broad, and I'm built like a motherfucking Sherman tank. Guys like this average height, narrow-chested Italian take one look at me and they see a great, lumbering force that, once within arms reach, will knock your fucking head off. They figure as long as they don't let me get close enough, they're safe, though. But they don't factor into the equation the fact that I am really fucking fast. I spend an hour a day sprinting on a goddamn treadmill. It's my job to be quick, unbelievably light on my feet, as I toss guy after guy around like ragdolls in the cage.

And so, this visitor from the Big Apple is about to get a lesson in humility. He's not likely to underestimate another of his opponents again, that's for sure.

"Why don't you take a second, Mr. Mayfair?" he says, flashing his teeth at me. "Think this through a little. Can't take back rash decisions, you know."

I'm done with talking to this guy. I'm done wasting breath telling him the same thing over and over again. I take a step to the right. The guy follows me with his gun, a hard light glinting in his eyes, as if he's seen the resolve in mine and recognized it for what it is—my absolute desire to cause him pain. He's watching my right hand, waiting for me to try and knock his weapon out of his hand with my left, so I can bring my fist crashing down into his face, but that's not what's about to happen.

I lunge, stepping in to him, raising my arm so that his wrist is between my ribcage and my bicep. Further. I step in further, and I bring my arm down, trapping him at the elbow between my arm and my chest.

"Motherfucker," he snarls, trying to spin the gun so he can shoot me with it, but he can't. He's locked at the joint, straining, trying to pull himself free of me. I can see in his eyes that he knows just how futile that course of action will be. His cigarette's dropped from his mouth, and it's now burning merrily between his body and mine, singeing a hole in my t-shirt, biting at the skin of my stomach. I'm sure it's burning him, too, but neither one of us move to angle our bodies away from one another. This is what they teach you when handling livestock: get too close for the animal to kick. If either of us twists our torsos away, we're giving the other the chance to strike at full force.

"You're dead," the Italian snaps. "You're just one man. You think you can defy the entire east coast mafia? You're a fucking lunatic."

I've never been one for shrugging. It's always seemed like such a half measure. I like to be decisive in my body language as well as in my words. Right now, a shrug seems to convey how little I fucking care about the east coast mafia, though. I hitch one shoulder, inching my face closer to the Italian's. "I defy anyone who tries to bend me to their will, asshole. I say to all comers, *Fuck. You.* I say try and kill me if you fucking dare."

My head comes crashing down on his. Even before I opened a fight gym and spent ninety percent of my day perfecting my MMA techniques, I knew how to deliver the perfect head butt. The flat of my forehead connects with his face, just above the bridge of his nose, right between the eyes, and blood explodes everywhere.

"*Jesus!*" The move takes him by surprise. A loud, ear-splitting crack tears the air in two behind me; he's fired the gun. Across the street, a dog starts howling. The Italian shuffles his feet, trying to plant one behind me so he can pitch me over his hip in a judo throw, but like I said...ain't my first time at the rodeo. While he's trying to

139

shimmy one leg past mine, struggling against me, I finally do hit him. I tighten my hand into a fist, raise it back as far as I can, maybe only five or six inches, and then I slam it down. I don't go for the face. The human skull, despite looking kind of fragile when stripped back, is actually really fucking strong. Its armor is designed to protect the brain, the most vital organ in the entire body, so of course it's going to be able to take a bit of a beating. The neck, on the other hand…

I land my fist straight into the Italian's trachea. I feel gristle and cartilage twist and crunch underneath my knuckles as I grind them into his neck. The Italian sags to the side, eyes bulging out of his head as he tries to get away, but I have a good hold on him now and I sure as shit ain't letting go. The gun goes off for a second time. I feel the bullet buzz my back, and I realize I've given my opponent a little too much room to maneuver in the scuffle. Time to fix that.

While he's choking, making unpleasant gurgling sounds, desperately trying to pull a meager breath of air through his crushed wind pipe, I release him, side step to the right, twist his arm before he can re-aim his weapon, and then I bring it down over my knee as hard as I can. I don't ease the intensity of the downward pressure I'm applying until I feel bone snap.

"*Arrrggghhhh!*" A string of expletives pours from the guy's mouth in Italian. His arm has broken with such force that I can see the jagged edge of his radius poking though the thin material of his shirt.

A dark satisfaction fills me from the tips of my toes to the roots of my hair. No way that's ever going to heal right. I didn't hear the Italian's gun clatter to the floor in amongst all of his screaming, but there it lays on the side walk, half kicked underneath the Denali, only the butt of the handle visible from where I'm standing. I reach down and scoop it up, while the man in front of me clutches at his arm with his good hand. His face is white with shock, aside from his nose and his mouth, which are covered in a river of blood.

"He's going to kill you for this. He's going to fucking *destroy* you!" the guy snarls.

"Whew. Apparently, he's already planning on killing me for turning down his offer. I've already earned my death twice today, and all before lunch. Big day for me, huh? Now, about that face..." I haven't used knuckle-dusters in a while. I haven't needed them; the bones in my fists are as strong as steel these days. So many hours spent smashing my fists into a speed bag (along with a number of people's faces) have conditioned them to be stronger than strong. I hold him by his crushed throat as I bring my fist down once, twice, three times. Each time I strike, the Italian makes a sick moaning noise, until the fourth hit, when he stops making noise at all.

The fucker's lost consciousness. I drop him to the ground and straighten, which is when I notice the woman on the other side of the street with a paper bag of groceries in her arms. She's stood stock still, frozen to the sidewalk, her mouth hanging open an inch as she stares at me with wide blue eyes. "I—I don't—I didn't—"

"Caught him trying to break into this house," I say, wiping my hands on my jeans. I toss the Italian's gun into the Denali through the broken driver's window, and then I proceed to collect the unconscious guy underneath the arms and drag him into the back seat. "Nothing to worry about now, ma'am. I've already called the cops. They're on their way to get him."

The woman shivers, clutching her groceries tighter, as if her onions, and her baking soda, and her Starbucks Chai Latte mix is enough to shield her from what she's witnessing. "Ri—right," she stammers. "Do you need me to stay? Or can I go?" she asks quietly. I can barely hear her.

"You should get home, ma'am. Make sure you're safe indoors. I'm sure this guy wasn't working alone."

She starts, like a jolt of electricity just fired through her. *There are more? There is an unknown number of violent, well-dressed Italian thieves in the neighborhood?* I can see the fear in her eyes. At some point, later on tonight maybe when she's had a chance to calm her nerves, she's going to second guess what I've told her and begin to think that something was amiss here. That maybe I wasn't the good Samaritan that I was claiming to be. That's if I'm lucky. She might get ten feet down the road and call the cops herself, just to make sure I wasn't lying, and then I'll really be screwed.

The woman hurries off, and I bundle the Italian into the back of the Denali, trying not to think about worst-case scenarios. How fucking stupid would it be if I got picked up for this? *Too* fucking stupid. I pull out my phone and jam it against the side of my head as I climb into the Denali and gun the engine. Michael picks up on the third ring.

"I need you to get out to Charlie's old place right now. I need you to come and get the Camaro."

"I assume you'll explain why later?"

"Sure. If I'm not in jail." I hang up, sliding my phone back into my pocket, and then I'm tearing through the streets of Hunt's Point, trying not to stick out like a sore thumb. Thankfully it's not that difficult. There are plenty of nice cars in this neighborhood, all the Richy Riches driving around in their Bugatti's and their Lambos, and so the Denali is actually pretty decent camouflage. As soon as I'm six blocks away, four blocks over from Charlie's place, I slow the fuck down, driving like all of the other retirees around here, too scared to scratch their nice cars.

About halfway back to the warehouse, the guy in the back begins to stir. I have to pull over at a gas station and climb in the back so I can restrain him. Thankfully, the Italian came prepared. God knows what he thought he was gonna fucking do to me, but there are zip ties and a fat roll of silver duct tape in the glove box, which comes in very handy. I wind the tape around his head three times just to make sure he has absolutely no chance of dislodging his gag, and then I double zip tie his hands behind his back, as well as at the ankles. No point in taking any risks. By the time I'm done fucking around, making sure he isn't going anywhere, the Italian is awake and shooting daggers at me. His sunglasses are on the floor at his feet, so I pick them up and place them back on his face, pinching his nose for good measure—must hurt like a motherfucker given how badly it's broken.

"Can't pack you up and put you on a plane back home, I'm afraid. You look like shit. Don't worry, though. I know a guy who'll have you back east in no time."

I do, too. When I reach the docks, I head straight for the harbormaster's office instead of stopping off at the warehouse first. I find Jeremy Daskill, fifty-three, sitting behind a desk piled with a mountain of paper with a glass of scotch firmly gripped in his meaty hand. He looks like he's seen a ghost when he looks up and lays eyes on me. This is always how he looks when I appear before him, ready with a favor to ask. Couple of years ago, I did Jeremy a favor of my own. His brother in law had gambled all of his sister's money away. He got drunk, beat and raped her, and then left her for dead at the foot of the stairs. Jeremy, good brother that he is, knew something needed to be done about the guy, so he came to me. The situation was dealt with, and now, whenever I need something stowed away in a shipping container for a while, or I need a bag or two dropped off into the Sound, I call on my friend Jeremy.

"Mr. Mayfair. Hi, I—I wasn't expecting you." Jeremy puts his scotch down behind a stack of papers, out of sight, like I would give a shit about him drinking while he's on the job. We all gotta do what we gotta do to get through.

"Hi there, Daskill." I give him a winning smile. "I have a little job I need you to do for me."

THIRTEEN

Mason

I spot Kaya in a booth on the far side of the café, sipping from a long, pink curly straw. She's drinking chocolate milk, of all things, and a metal cup is sitting next to her tall glass on the table, sweating with condensation. When she sees me enter, the bell hanging above the door chiming loudly to announce the arrival of another customer, she takes another bendy straw out of a caddy resting up against the wall—green this time—and she drops it into the silver cup, pushing it across the table so that it's directly in front of me when I sit down.

"It's almost nine," she says, tracing her finger in a patch of water on the table. She makes a flower. "I thought you weren't going to come."

"I had to finish something up at the shop." The Impala took longer than I thought it would, but I managed to get it done. When I told Mac what I'd done—a feat not even he could have accomplished—he relieved me of the keys and grunted under his breath, slamming his office door in my face. Asshole.

"Get you anything, sweetie?" A short woman with insanely tight curls hovers by the table, notepad in hand, pencil raised and ready to record my every desire. I order a coffee and she looks disappointed, like my dreams should have been bigger. Kaya doesn't say anything about the fact that I'm not drinking her proffered chocolate milk.

"I need to make this quick. My sister's with a sitter and it's her first night home after the hospital," I tell her.

Kaya blinks at me like a very wise owl. "You're not going to like this."

"I already don't like it. You've got me freaked out. I feel like I've done something wrong." I can't have done something wrong, though. I'm not dating Kaya. I haven't slept with her. I sure as fuck haven't slept with her and then slept with her best friend, so what's going on? Why the hell is she looking at me across the table with such worry in her eyes?

"It's about my brother," she says.

"Your *brother*?" I haven't looked sideways at Jameson Rayne. *Ever*. Giving Jameson any reason to think I'm interested in absolutely anything he does is tantamount to inviting an ass kicking like no other.

Kaya nods. "Yeah. Jameson. Not just him, though. It's

about your friend Ben, too."

Ah. Now that makes more sense. Ben's been getting himself into trouble ever since we were kids. He's managed to keep his head down for the last little while, though. It should be no surprise that his well-behaved run is finally at an end.

"What the fuck has he done?" I sit back, settling into my seat. I'm not going to be able to drain my coffee and run after all.

"He and Jameson were stupid. Jameson makes deals with fighters sometimes. He's pretty arrogant. He knows he's a good fighter. Great, even. So when he's matched against an opponent by Johnny and his guys at French's, he'll go find them a few days before. He'll offer them a percentage of his winnings if the other guy agrees to go down in a specific round, in a specific way. No one's ever not taken the deal. I mean, they're not stupid. They know already they're going to lose. So they always take the money and go down when he tells them to."

"Wait. So all these guys are throwing their fights?" My stomach has contorted itself into a knot of unbelievable intricacy. It's going to take a miracle to untangle it. Throwing fights, even in small time underground matches like the ones held at French's, is a heinous crime in the eyes of any organizer. And organizers are usually violent, unforgiving men with a penchant for breaking people's kneecaps with a sledgehammer should the mood take them.

"Jesus. Keep your voice down." Kaya takes a drink from her milkshake, scanning the room to see if anyone's listening. I already know we're the only ones in here, but she seems on edge. Frightened, even. I can't say I blame her. The waitress brings me a mug filled to the brim with filter coffee blacker than tar. When she's gone, I lean across the table to hiss out my next question under my breath.

"*Tell me Ben wasn't stupid enough...*" I already know he was, though, otherwise Kaya wouldn't be here, telling me this.

"He took five grand to go down in the first round. Jameson wanted it to look like he'd destroyed him, and your friend said he needed the cash. Extra, if Jameson wanted to humiliate him in the ring. So that's what happened. And then this morning three of the doormen from French's show up at the apartment and drag him out of bed. They said they knew about what he and Ben had done. Told him it would be better for him if he just admitted it. Jameson said he didn't know what the fuck they were talking about, but they obviously knew he was lying. They tried to beat the shit out of him, but you know my brother."

He put up a fight. Of course he did; it's in his very nature to brawl. And if he had three guys looming over him after he'd just been rudely awoken from sleep, I'm imagining it was in Jameson Rayne's nature to knock all of their fucking teeth out. Kaya continues.

"He broke one of their collar bones for sure. The bone was sticking out of his neck," she whispers. Her face is devoid of all color, her skin ashen. "There was blood everywhere. I was screaming at them to leave then, to just go, but the other two guys lost it. They said he could fuck one of them up, but he had no chance against two of them together."

"Let me guess. He snapped their bones like twigs, too."

"He smashed one of their faces into the cook top. It dented the metal. He shoved the other one out of a second story window. He landed on his back. I have no idea whether he lived or died. I kept trying to lean out of the window to look, but Jameson wouldn't let me. He was still screaming at the other two, trying to make them leave, so I stood well back and prayed it was going to be over soon. Before they went, the main doorman guy, the one with the shaved head and the knuckle tattoos—" I know the one she's talking about "—told him it was only a matter of time. They knew what he'd done, and they knew Ben was in on it, too. They said Ben wouldn't be able to hide the truth, and that the two of them were dead men walking. They can't have gone to find Ben straight away, they were far too messed up, but that's not to say the guys at French's didn't send someone else over to speak to your friend."

"Why the fuck didn't you tell me he was in trouble at the shop?" I snap. My voice is raised, drawing attention from the curly haired woman watching an old re-run of Jerry Springer on the ancient, fuzzy television behind the counter. I know I've been a shit immediately. I didn't give her a chance to tell me earlier. I was rude and I chased her away before she had the chance to tell me anything whatsoever. Kaya's ears pull back a little, her eyes narrowing.

"I don't need to be here right now, Mason. I could be at home, sweeping up broken glass and trying to glue the shattered remains of my furniture back together. Instead I thought I would give you a heads up. Jameson told me he would deal with it, but I know when my brother's lying, okay? Ben doesn't matter to him. If those doormen are too distracted hunting down your friend and beating the shit out of him, Jameson has time to figure out a way to get back into their good graces at French's. He'd kill me if he knew I was here. So, please, Mason. Cut me some slack."

"You're right. I'm sorry. I'm really sorry." I rub my hands over my face, blowing out a deep breath. Fuck. How the hell am I going to fix *this*? I'm a no one in the fighting world. I don't have anyone's ear to whisper into. I don't have any favors to call in. I mean, I have absolutely no way of digging Ben out of this hole he's managed to fall into. So fucking typical. I feel like I've been doing this my entire fucking life. "Thank you for letting me know," I say quietly. Outside on the street, a police siren blares into life right outside the coffee shop, drowning out my words. Both Kaya and I startle at the sound. The car races off down the street, tires audibly screeching as it takes a corner too fast, leaving both myself and the tiny woman opposite me smiling nervously for no good reason.

"You should find him," Kaya says. "These guys aren't known to wait around."

"I know. I will. And your brother—"

"Don't worry about my brother. Jameson's like a goddamn cat with nine hundred lives. This time next week, he'll be the golden boy at French's again. And if not, the heavies who run the fights will all be dead and Jameson'll be living in their houses, fucking their wives, and their kids will be calling him daddy. He always lands on his feet, you know? But your friend..."

I nod, staring at my coffee. She's right. Ben *never* lands on his feet. Ben has the worst luck in the whole fucking world.

FOURTEEN

Sloane

I've lost count of the times I've been afraid over the past year. I don't seem to recall a week where I haven't had reason to be afraid. Okay, since Charlie Holsan died and Zeth took over the gym, things have quietened down, but even that quiet has been punctuated with spells of panic. You ask yourself, how long can this possibly last? How much time will pass before something terrible happens? Before the grim reaper comes knocking on your door. I know better than that; the grim reaper doesn't knock. He sneaks into your house, unbidden, without your knowledge or consent. He takes without asking, and there is absolutely nothing you can do about it. But still, it doesn't stop you from trying to hold back disaster. You still end up with your back pressed up against the door, heels digging into the ground, trying to prevent the inevitable.

I thought I'd reached the limit, maxed out the human capacity to experience fear, and yet as I stare down at the slender piece of plastic in my hands, eyes fixed on the brazen pink + sign filling the tiny display window, I know a pure and paralyzing fear the likes of which I've never encountered before.

Pregnant?

How the fuck can I be *pregnant*?

I know the answer to that very obvious question: I was sick. I took antibiotics that screwed with my birth control, and then I had wild, animalistic sex with my boyfriend, and he came deep inside me. I remember the particular incident all too well. But that's not what I'm asking. How could fate have permitted such a thing to happen? How could the universe have stood by and let life spark and form inside me, when I am who I am, a woman constantly balancing on the precipice of danger? A woman in love with a man who will probably end up shot and killed someday? I knew what I was getting myself into when I allowed myself to fall for Zeth. I was all too aware of the dangers and the risks, and I accepted them all because the reward of loving him was far greater than the fear of losing him. But this little baby inside me? This baby doesn't have a fucking clue who its father is. It doesn't know who its mother is, either. It didn't get to choose us, the way I chose Zeth. It seems outrageous that such a tragic thing has been allowed to come to pass.

My eyes have misted over. I don't know how long I lean up against the wall of the bathroom, staring at the pregnancy test in my hands, but when I finally manage to pull myself together my shoulder is aching like a bitch and my eyes feel very dry, like I haven't blinked in a really long time. I want to cry. I want to dash over to the hospital and grab another three tests so I can do them all again, praying as I wait for each result to develop that the first was wrong somehow. It would be a waste of time, though. I know the test isn't wrong. The body doesn't lie. As if to prove that point, my stomach heaves and roils as I hurry out of the bathroom and downstairs into the kitchen. The house is filled with an oppressive silence, as though the walls were inhaling and exhaling a little while ago but now they have stopped, now holding their breath, now waiting for what comes next.

I have no fucking clue what comes next.

Ernie raises his head as I enter the kitchen. The small nub of his docked tail slides back and forth on the tile like a windscreen wiper as he watches me pour myself a glass of water from the tap and down it in one go. He makes a comical yowling sound, little schnauzer eyebrows raised, head angled to one side, like he's trying to ask me what's wrong.

"I'll tell you what's wrong, buddy. Everything is fucking wrong. The shit is about to hit the fucking fan, my little furry friend, and I have no idea what the fuck

I'm going to fucking do about it." Ernie doesn't understand my need to swear in continued succession; he opens his mouth and begins to pant. It looks like he's laughing. "This is not funny," I tell him.

I should eat something. I haven't had anything in my stomach for hours and I'm feeling a little light headed, but I know as soon as I get something down it'll be coming right back up again. I've seen so many pregnant women in my time at St. Peter's. Most of them suffer from morning sickness, and there are a lucky few who don't. The women who *do* suffer from the constant need to throw up seem to bear it with rueful pride. *Look at me. I'm so pregnant, I just can't seem to stop voiding the contents of my stomach everywhere.* It doesn't seem as though any of them have ever been *this* sick, though. I can't get up out of a chair without wanting to run for the bathroom. And don't get me started on bacon. The faintest whiff of greasy, salty, usually delicious bacon, and I can feel the bile rising like a tidal wave up my esophagus. It's getting harder and harder to disguise the fact that I'm not sick with the flu, and that I am, in fact, very knocked up.

Oh my god. What the hell am I going to tell my parents? I was supposed to be married and settled down with a nice neurosurgeon when I started a family. I wasn't supposed to be living in sin with an ex-hit man. It doesn't really matter what Mom and Dad think at this point, though. It only matters what one person thinks about it, and I'm almost one hundred percent sure I know how he's going to react when he finds out.

He's going to lose his goddamn mind. I can't imagine him as a father. I can't picture it at all. I've tried not to picture how it's going to go when I tell him, because I'm too damn scared to even think about it, but when the scenario has pushed its way into my head despite my best efforts to keep it at bay, things have not gone well. Furniture has been smashed. Angry words have been thrown. Tears have been shed. I've imagined him saying the very worst things to me, his anger spiked, his eyes filled with misery. I haven't, on the other hand, been able to imagine what I'm doing while Zeth is losing his shit. Am I happy that he's horrified by the idea of a child? Am I glad that he doesn't want it? Am I relieved that I don't need to go through with becoming a mother? Or...

I'm too scared to consider the *or*.

If I'm not happy or relieved, then it means that I'm heartbroken, and that possibility doesn't even bear thinking about. I can't have a baby. I can't be pregnant and carry a child to term. I'm not ready. I've never even thought about a family with Zeth, not even in an abstract, whimsical way, because such a thing is an impossibility. This life that we live together, it's not safe for *us*, let alone another vulnerable, innocent human being. It wouldn't be fair. It would be *cruel*.

And yet, a shade of doubt...

A what if...

Sloane Romera: Doctor.

Sloane Romera: Accomplice.

Sloane Romera: Lover.

Sloane Romera: Mother?

The idea sits heavy on my shoulders, either a weighty responsibility, or a weighty blessing. I just—I just don't fucking know!

"Stop looking at me like that, Ernie." His eyes are shining bright, his face lit up with the simple joy of attention being paid to him, but to me it looks like he's happy that these sneaky thoughts are infiltrating my brain. "You're supposed to be on my side," I tell him. He gets up and comes to me, raising his head so he can rest his chin against my kneecap, looking up at me with those deep, soulful brown eyes of his. Sometimes it seems as though he's wiser than most people I meet in the street. He manages to communicate so much in that even, steady gaze of his.

"I'm not telling him," I say. "There's no way I can tell him."

Ernie blinks.

"I *can't*. You don't understand. How could you?"

The tip of the dog's tongue uncurls from his mouth, poking through his teeth, and then disappearing again. "It's not that simple. Pregnancies fail sometimes, you know. It would be stupid to say something this early. Who knows? It might not take, and then the arguing, the fighting, it will all have been for nothing."

Ernie makes a disapproving grumble at the back of his throat.

"I'm waiting at least a month," I say, imbuing my voice with a certainty that I'm definitely not feeling. "A month is fair. A month isn't long."

Ernie's eyebrows twitch again, his eyes locked onto me, his tail still madly flicking back and forth. He doesn't have a clue what I'm talking about, but for some reason I get the feeling he disapproves. "Look, it's not up to you, anyway. It's up to me. I need time to process this, okay? And looking at me like that isn't going to change anything."

The sound of the front door opening nearly causes my heart to explode. I panic, hands patting myself down, searching for something...for the pregnancy test. Did I bring it down here with me? Is it still upstairs in the bathroom? What the fuck did I do with it? My hand finds the length of plastic in my jeans, barely managing to fit all the way into the pocket at my hip. I shove it down as hard as I can, pulling at my t-shirt then, hoping the material covers the pocket from view altogether, as if my boyfriend has laser eyesight and might be able to see through the denim of my jeans. Zeth appears, and all the oxygen leaves my lungs.

He's covered in blood.

"What—what the hell happened?" I can't seem to find my voice.

He props himself up against the wall, looking down at

himself. "Well. I was driving across town and I realized I was being followed. I thought it was Lowell, but turns out it was the Italians. Got a little ugly."

"The Italians? The guys from New York?" I remember them calling a couple of weeks ago. Seemed like they wouldn't quit for a while there. It's been quiet for long enough since then that I thought the bastards had given up harassing him and had decided to leave him the fuck alone. Really, how stupid is an assumption like that? What the hell is wrong with me? Being sick and dealing with this Mason crap has really blindsided me.

"What happened exactly? What—what did you do with him?" I hate to ask questions like this, but I need to know.

Zeth proceeds to describe in intricate detail how he restrained the guy after breaking his nose and drove him across town to the docklands, where he had some guy he knows seal the Italian's car with him inside it into a shipping container back to New York. It's going to take three days for the container to reach it's destination, by which time the mafia guy inside the corrugated metal is going to have lost his fucking mind. I can't see how this is going to end well. On top of everything else? Jesus, it'll be a wonder if any of us make it through the next month.

"I didn't want to tell you." Zee pushes away from the wall, yanking his blood stained t-shirt over his head in one rough, incredibly sexy move. "But...y'know. No secrets," he says gruffly. I love that he wants me to know everything. Being kept in the dark so much back when we first met, along with more recently, when he was hiding Lowell's arrival, was infuriating and also very dangerous, and so the fact that he wants me clued in these days is reassuring. But damn if the guy doesn't know how to make a girl feel like utter crap.

He says no secrets, and I have the biggest secret of my life nestled up, snug and warm in my uterus. Fuck. I should tell him. I should tell him right fucking now. I'm going to do it. I have to. I can't *not* tell him. I—

He cups my face in his hands, and his knuckles are covered in *blood.* I can smell it on him, thick, coppery, overpowering. My stomach heaves. "Okay, angry girl? You look...kinda pale," he says. I love the look of concern he wears. Those deep brown eyes are brimming over with it as he rubs his thumbs over my cheeks. "Aren't you supposed to be at work today?"

I shake my head, touching my fingertips to his wrists. If he doesn't remove them soon, the smell of the blood is going to make me vomit. "I was meant to. I still didn't feel well, though." *Please, dear lord, don't let him think it's weird that I'm still sick. Please!* "I have plenty of unused vacation time, so I figured why not take the rest of the week off. HR were threatening to make me take enforced leave, so this kinda works out for everybody."

Zeth studies me for a moment with sharp, intelligent eyes. Slowly, so painfully slowly, he leans down, his face getting closer and closer as the seconds pass. I imagine him calling me out on my half-truth. It feels so shitty not telling him what's going on after I gave him hell for not telling me about Lowell only a few days ago. Is it obvious that I'm hiding something? Is my fear and panic sitting there on my face, out in the open for him to see, plain as day? It has to be; I don't know how I could possibly hide it.

Zeth's lips part. He's going to say something. He's going to say something...

He kisses me.

I'm so surprised by the soft, gentle pressure of his lips grazing mine, barely making contact, that I feel all power draining from my arms and my legs. I melt into him, my chest meeting his, and he wraps his arms around me, crushing me against him. My breath leaves my lungs in a long sigh. I can feel Zeth's lips form the shape of a smile as he grins savagely against me. The tip of his tongue flicks out between his teeth, tracing it gently over my lips, and then deeper, over *my* teeth. It's ridiculous how quickly my body betrays me. My head swims as he envelops me, and the anxiety of the last few moments, hell, of the entire morning, is drifting away like so much smoke.

Worlds are miraculously created and come to catastrophic ends in the brief minute where Zeth Mayfair holds me in his arms. The universe sighs at the beauty of it all. When he pulls back, Zeth's irises are flashing, filled with steel. "You have nothing to worry about, angry girl. You know that, don't you? The Italians are just stretching their legs, pushing to see how hard I push back. If they want Seattle, they can come and take it. They're not going to get any trouble from me. I told them I'm done. I won't ever be someone else's whipping boy again. And I won't involve myself in shit that might ever take me away from you. Nothing in the world is worth that."

So he has seen my panic. He's mistaken it for something else, though. Makes sense that I'd be upset about how his day has panned out so far; I don't correct him. I smile weakly, feeling like I'm betraying him as I turn away, reaching under the sink for the small first aid kit I keep there.

I unzip the small red bag and reach for the alcohol wipes inside. "I know. I'm sorry. I shouldn't be worried. I know everything's going to be okay. I guess—I guess I'm just being stupid. Here, let me clean those hands up."

Zeth grunts as I apply the alcohol wipes to his split knuckles. This part of our day is practically routine now, given how often he messes up his hands at the gym. It doesn't escape me that somewhere leaving Seattle, a shipping container is headed for New York with an irate Italian trapped inside, though. That part of our day is definitely different.

Zeth is quiet, watching me with a quiet, all too familiar intensity as I go about my task. I may have told him a moment ago that I know everything is going to be okay, but from my shaky delivery down to the tremble in my hands, I know I didn't do a very good job convincing him that I'm okay. His body takes on that strange, intimidating stillness that always arrives when he's thinking too hard. I look up at him, smiling, trying to ease the tension around my eyes some, but I know it's too late for that now. He folds his arms around me, drawing me into a long hug. Trying to hide this thing is going to be difficult, and it's only going get harder.

He knows something is up.

FIFTEEN

Mason

Lack of sleep really fucks up my schedule. I spent all night trying to locate Ben, calling around everyone I could think of, trying to track him down, but the bastard's disappeared from the face of the earth and no one seems to know where the hell he is. If they do, they're not telling, anyway. Millie had a coughing fit in the night which scared me half to death, so I spent the remainder of the dark hours sitting in a chair beside her bed, watching her sleep, watching her little chest rise and fall, the soft sounds of her breathing filling the room, which explains why I feel like a goddamn zombie as I pull up outside work in the morning. I'm on time—a minor miracle in itself—but I can tell Mac's still pissed at me when I climb out of the truck.

"What's up, Mac?" I slam the car door, bracing for the

stream of abuse he's obviously about to hurl at me. I know things are serious when Dave appears from out back and plants himself against a workbench, arms folded across his chest, jaw locked, with a severe look on his face. Dave used to work on engines like me, but recently he's spent less and less time turning up for morning shifts, instead appearing as the sun is going down, picking up tools when I'm putting them down. I have no idea what Mac has him doing, but it's not legal and it's bound to get him into serious shit some point soon.

When he reaches me, Mac slaps his palms against my chest, grabbing hold of my t-shirt. "Get your ass out back, you little punk. You an' me are gonna have a little chat."

Fuck. What the hell is this about? Any number of scenarios flash through my mind. Maybe he did see Kaya show up yesterday. Maybe he's heard about me training over with Zeth. I quickly discover it's neither of those things, though. It's way, way worse. Mac corrals me through the narrow doorway and out into the yard behind the shop. The ground is littered with spent cigarette butts and shattered pieces of brick. Mac picks up one of the larger pieces of brick at his feet and tosses it up in the air, catching it in the flat of his palm. "You had an early morning visitor today, Mason. Someone who seemed very interested in catching you before you started work."

"Oh?" I try not to eyeball the brick. I get the feeling I'll be getting a very close look at it soon enough.

"Yeah. *Oh*. This early morning caller said she was a friend of yours. I saw you talking to her a couple of weeks back, talking to her outside the shop, and you told me she was just asking for directions. Remember?"

Of course I remember. I remember all too well. The very first time I met Lowell, she pulled up in her bland sedan with the tinted out windows, and she spent the next five minutes explaining in great detail how she was going to fuck with my shit if I didn't help her. Mac had asked me about it the next day, suspicion deeply engrained in every line of his body, and I'd told him she was just some tourist, asking how to get to the Pacific Science Center. "No. No, I can't say that I do," I lie.

"Well, she seems to know you, Mason. She said she'd been trying to get hold of you for a couple of days now. Said she hadn't had any joy. And this woman, she said something really interesting before she left, Mason. You wanna know what she said?"

I keep my tongue in my head. Nothing I can do or say is going to make this situation any better. The wisest course of action is to seal my mouth shut and wait it out, see what happens. Mac throws the brick. It launches through the air and impacts with the wall just behind my head, exploding into tiny chunks of debris and a cloud of red dust.

"She said you weren't holding up your end of the

bargain. That you hadn't *given her anything interesting in days.*" Mac shrugs, his palms turned up to the early morning sky. It looks like it's going to rain. Why the fuck I'm noticing something so arbitrary as the weather when Mac looks like he's about to cut my fucking head off is beyond me, but I can't help it. "Why the fuck would this woman show up here, talking about you *giving her something interesting*? Tell me, Mason, 'cause I am all out of ideas over here."

"I don't know. I don't know what the fuck you're talking about." Probably shouldn't have said something so patently untrue. Mac snarls under his breath, reaching down to pick up another brick. This time it hits home. Pain blossoms like a firework in my head as the chunk of stone smashes into my left shoulder.

"You lying little shit. You've been informing on us this whole fucking time!" Mac screams. "I kept asking myself over and over, why the fuck won't this kid pick up any extra work? Why won't he just give in and fucking take the easy route? And now this...*this* makes everything so much clearer. Can't be blurring the lines between right and wrong, picking up extra work, if you're already working for the *cops* now, can you?" Another brick flies through the air. Dave stands off to one side, watching on with grim satisfaction as Mac volleys missile after missile at my head. "She even left her fucking card for you in case you'd lost her number, you ungrateful little *cunt*!" Mac rips a rectangular flash of white card from the top pocket of his shirt and flicks it at me; it falls at my feet in the bare dirt, but I can see all too well the blocky black print on its surface:

Denise Lowell
Drug Enforcement Agency

Why the fuck would she do this? Coming here? To the shop? She must be furious with me if she thinks betraying me to Mac, letting him in on the fact that I've been feeding her information, is going to make me comply with her wishes. Her actions are more likely to get me fucking killed. Lowell knows Mac's up to all sorts of shady shit here once the roller shutters are pulled closed each night. The stolen cars that get shunted through Mac's are innumerable. She has to know he would assume I was informing on *him* if she did this; it must have been her plan all along.

Fuck that fucking bitch.

If I ever see her again…

But, no. I probably won't see her again. The likelihood of me seeing *anyone* ever again is pretty fucking slim. Mac has this look in his eye—pure hatred, so intense and so raw that it looks like it's gripped him whole. I won't be walking out of here today. I'm going to be bundled into the trunk of one of Mac's cars, and he's going to have my body dumped on the stairs of the downtown police station. A message to those who think they can snitch on someone like Mac and get away with it.

"I haven't told her anything about you, Mac. What the fuck could I have told her? I don't *know* anything. Please, Mac. Just think this through." It's barely worth wasting my breath, but I have to try. I'm a proud guy. I hate to make myself look weak, hate begging, but a responsibility like mine will make a guy do all kinds of things. Millie is the only thing that matters. If I'm not there to take care of her, who the fuck will? She'll be placed into the foster care system, and what family is going to want to take care of a six-year-old who suffers from grand mal seizures? No one, that's who.

Mac snorts, looking at Dave. "Can you believe this shit? It's fucking pathetic. Why else would a fucking DEA bitch show up here, spouting shit like that, if it weren't true?"

Mac is many things, but smart is not one of them. "Why the fuck would she show up here, spouting that shit, if it *was* true? God, Mac! If I were an informant, working for her to try and bring you down, she would have just blown my cover and ruined her whole operation by talking to you. She would never have done it!"

A shadow of doubt flickers over Mac's otherwise angry features. I've got him thinking, but it won't be enough. I know it won't. Men like Mac don't spare another man's life on the off chance they could be wrong about them. They kill them with their own bare hands in case they're *right.*

"Then you deny knowing her?" he spits. "You've never met her in your entire life?"

"I've met her. She's blackmailing me into helping her. It has nothing to do with you, though."

"Bullshit."

"It's the truth. They found some dead body up in the mountains. They're trying to pin the murder on the guys across the street."

"On Mayfair?" Mac looks dubious. No doubt he has a fair few bodies of his own buried in the mountains that border the city. His mind is probably screaming at him, trying to recall when and where the other victims of his rage were all disposed of. "No one would be stupid enough to fuck with Mayfair. Not even the DEA," he snaps. "If you're gonna lie, you little fuck, you'd better come up with something slightly more believable."

I bang the back of my head against the wall behind me, gritting my teeth. How the hell do you make a mad man see sense? Mac can be pretty reasonable when the mood takes him, but when he's fired up and out for blood like this, sense isn't any good to him, and therefore it's banished from reach until later when cooler heads prevail.

"They have history," I say. "She's been after him for a while now. Go and ask him. Go and ask Zeth about her, for fuck's sake. He'll tell you it's true."

"Ha! No fucking way. So you're saying he knows

about this bitch trying to pinch him for murder?"

I nod.

"There is no fucking way on this earth a man like him would know about her and she would be still drawing breath. Just no way. He's old school. He's one of Charlie Holsan's boys. He's like me. You don't leave problems like that walking around, causing trouble, creating problems for you. You take care of them immediately and have done with it."

Out of the corner of my eye, Dave is shifting uncomfortably from foot to foot. He's hovering in the doorway, keeping an eye out for people approaching the shop from the street, while at the same time remaining close to help Mac if I become too much of a problem. Right now, he looks distinctly uncomfortable, like he has something to say but can't quite bring himself to say it.

Mac spits onto the ground, stooping slowly to collect up another brick. He passes it from one hand to the other, coldly regarding me with distaste. "Maybe killing you isn't enough, Reeves. After all the shit I've done for you, all the slack I've given you, you do *this* to *me*?" Shaking his head violently from side to side, he grunts, narrowing his eyes. "No. Killing you won't be enough. Maybe Dave will go pay a visit to Millie after we're done here. Seems like a kindness to me, in fact. Put the poor little bitch out of her misery once and for all. What do you say, Mase? You think we'd be doing her a favor?"

My body reacts without my permission. I fly at the

old man, fists raised, and I hit him hard. His head kicks back, blood spattering everywhere as his nose makes a wet popping sound.

"Ho shit," Dave whispers. "You did *not* just do that."

I'm not listening to him, though. I'm deaf and I am blind to anything but the man lying on the ground before me. He can't be allowed to hurt her. He just can't be allowed to fucking hurt her. No matter what, I have to make sure Mac never comes within three fucking feet of Millie. Something's in my hand, something uneven and rough against my already rough skin: a heel of shattered brick. That will do. When Mac was launching the bricks at me just now, he wasn't really aiming properly. He was trying to scare me, to get me to admit to something that would damn me. When I throw the brick, I'm aiming right between the bastard's eyes. He sees it coming way too late. Mac screams as the brick makes contact, holding his hands over his face. I don't stop there, though. I pick up another brick, and another and another, throwing each one as hard as I can at his head until his hands fall away and his flesh is a bloody, messy pulp.

I can hear nothing but the loud rush of my blood hurtling through me.

And then:

"Mason? Mason! Jesus fucking Christ, man, stop! You're going to kill him!" Dave's hands are all over me, tearing at my clothes, trying to get me to still myself, but

I'm gripping by a power larger and stronger than myself. Dave isn't a small guy, and yet it takes him a long time to pin my arms to my side. "Fuck, Mase, he wasn't gonna kill ya. You know he wasn't."

"Bullshit! He would have done it and he wouldn't have fucking thought twice. You were gonna stand there and watch him do it, you sick fuck!" I rip myself free of him and spin, shoving him away from me. "Don't fucking touch me. Don't you fucking dare!"

Dave looks stunned. Mac's unconscious on the floor, and his breathing is labored. His nose is shattered, and the index finger on his left hand is practically hanging off, skin scraped away so badly that the bone is exposed beneath. "Shit, Mason. You really fucked him up. You think he's gonna go easy on you now? You're a fucking mad man!"

"I don't care if he goes easy on me, man. Let him come for me again. I'll finish the job next time." If I stand here any longer, Dave's going to gather his wits and grab hold of me before I can make a run for it. I push past him, ready to turn and fight again if I have to, but Mac's coughing and spluttering all of a sudden, making pathetic groaning noises, and Dave rushes to his side, calling his name.

My eyes don't see straight until I'm halfway across the street, my feet already marching on a direct route toward the gym. The place is locked up, though. The shutters are down. I can easily get in, sure, but if Zee or

Michael aren't there then what's the point?

I turn back and jump into my truck, speeding away down the street before anything else can turn to shit. I don't know where I'm going, but I do know one thing: I'm no longer safe. My life is in danger, and it's all Lowell's fault. I'm gonna make her pay. I'm gonna make her pay for what she's done.

••••

It's late. I spent the afternoon trying to track down Ben again—this time for my sake as much as his own. No joy, though. He seems to have disappeared off the face of the planet, and I can't help but worry that maybe the guys at French's have caught up with him already.

I have more luck with Lowell. Following the string of aggressive text messages I send through to the burner phone I know she always keeps in the pocket of her pantsuit, I finally receive a response:

2134 W Renshaw

That's all it says. The first line of an address. I plug the information into my cell phone and pull up a route to the location, and then I burn across there, my hands itching like crazy as I try to strangle the steering wheel. The address, as it turns out, is an innocuous looking drug store on the outskirts of town—a twenty-four hour place that seems to sell everything and nothing all at once. I find Denise in the feminine hygiene isle.

"So you're on your period? Is that why you just destroyed my fucking life?" I grab hold of her by the shoulders, shoving her roughly. She staggers sideways into a shelving unit stacked high with pink and purple brightly colored packs of...of god knows what. At the far end of the aisle, a young woman with a ponytail, wearing a set of green overalls looks up, eyes filled with judgment.

"Careful," Lowell advises, straightening her suit. "Don't want to rile the natives. Wouldn't go down well."

"You're one sick bitch, you know that?" I want to knock her fucking head off, but smashing Lowell's skull will come with a set of consequences, just like beating the crap out of Mac will. Assaulting Lowell ends only one way: with me serving a very long sentence in a very dangerous prison. I have to squeeze my hands into fists, digging my fingernails into my palms in order to stop myself from unleashing on her. "I'm not sure what you wanted to happen when you decided to go over to Mac's place, but you'll be happy to know I've basically got a contract out on my head, I've lost my job, and I'm going to have to pull Millie out of school so those sick bastards don't try and kill her, too. Are you happy? Are you fucking happy?"

Lowell brushes her hair behind her ears. She normally wears it scraped back close to her scalp, but today her shoulder length blonde hair is free. It makes

SAVAGE THINGS

her less severe somehow. I'd be a fool to be tricked by
this simple slight of hand, though. She's just about as
severe as they get, and she's proud of the fact. "If there's
one thing you ought to know about me, Mr. Reeves, it's
that I'm only ever happy when I'm chasing down a felon.
You made me very unhappy when you failed to provide
any information on Mayfair. So in return, I made you
very unhappy. That's how this arrangement works,
okay?"

"Not okay." I lean in, hissing, so only she can hear me.
"I just lost all means of keeping my sister clothed and fed
with a roof over her head. Do you have any idea what
you've done?"

"Yes, I do. I've motivated you, Mason." She reaches
into the inside pocket of her suit jacket and removes a
white envelope. Pressing it against my chest, she raises
both eyebrows. "One week's wages. Not enough to grow
complacent on, but enough to pay some bills. If you want
more money, you need to give me something I can work
with. Give me something great that means I can put Zeth
where he belongs and I'll give you six month's wages.
How long could you take care of Millie with that? Pay for
her meds? Keep her in Pokémon, or whatever kids are
playing with these days." She gives me a pointed look.
"You see, I can be quite benevolent when the mood takes
me. But I can also throw whoever the fuck I want under
the bus if it means I get closer to accomplishing my goal.
Understand?"

Shit. She's made it virtually impossible for me to do anything but play ball with her. I take the envelope from her and look inside. There are seven crisp one hundred dollar bills inside—I don't know what she thought Mac was paying me but she's just given me a fifty percent pay raise. I consider the notes tucked inside the envelope, trying to figure out how to make this right, but I can't. The bitch owes me. She took away my livelihood, she owes me big time. And yet the money is dirty, feels dirty, makes *me* feel dirty. I want to throw it back in her face.

Instead I slip it into my back pocket.

"I'll get you what you're looking for," I tell her. "It doesn't seem like you've given me much of a choice."

Lowell smiles a smug, terrible smile that makes me feel sick to my stomach. "Good boy, Mason. I'm so pleased you've come to your senses."

I leave the drug store before I can go on the hunt for something caustic enough to kill her. I need to know Millie's safe. Mac's going to be on the warpath—if he's alive, of course—and he's going to be looking for revenge. He's a sick fuck. No doubt about it, he'd take his anger out on a child if the opportunity arose. He knows I leave my sister with a sitter, but thankfully I've never mentioned who I leave her with. I call Wanda, and she confirms that Millie's safe and sound, a little tired but doing just fine.

The key's in the truck's ignition, ready to be turned, and my hand is on the gear stick, ready to throw it into drive, when I see Lowell flit out of the drug store and cross the street, running toward a fairly unassuming blue SUV, the kind so generic that you barely notice them among the sea of other generic SUVs that flood the roads. She hops in the front driver's seat and straps herself in, and the whole time, my mind is ticking. Tick, tick, ticking. I don't know when I decide to follow her. It's not really a conscious decision. It's only when I'm pulling up outside a modest two story building in Greenwood and Lowell goes inside that I realize what I've done. Fuck me. If she saw me tailing her, I'm in for a world of hurt. I was careful, though. I made sure to move a few cars back, never in the same lane of traffic unless absolutely necessary.

Lights go on inside the house. Movement: a dark shadow shifts from one room to the next, and then the hall and upstairs lights go on. Lowell appears at the window for a second, a coffee cup in her hand. She draws one curtain closed across the glass in front of her, and then the other. For all the world, it looks like Denise Lowell just arrived home and is settling in for the night.

And now I know where she lives.

SIXTEEN

Sloane

"How the fuck could you be so reckless?" Oliver pulls off his rubber gloves and hurls them into the HAZMAT bin by the door. "I—I don't even know what to say, Sloane. I just can't...fucking...believe..."

I knew he wasn't going to react well, but I had no idea I was going to render him speechless. The blood test he's just performed has confirmed once and for all that I'm pregnant, and he is none too happy about the revelation. "Have you thought about your options?" he asks. His back is to me, so I can't see the look on his face. I can picture it, though: so much disappointment and worry there.

"My options?" I know all too well what he's talking about. Have I thought about if I want to keep the baby, or if I want to take another route? Have a termination. I've thought about both options endlessly, but admitting this to Oliver feels wrong somehow. He sighs, his shoulders dropping. Turning around, he leans back against the desk behind him, crossing his arms over his chest.

"Don't, Sloane. Just don't. It's an insult to my intelligence. Let me help you out with your decision. You know as well as I do that you're in the peak of your career. Do you think you're still going to be able to specialize if you're pregnant? Working the trauma floor is exhausting at the best of times. And once you have the baby, then what? You think you're gonna be able to run yourself into the ground, working sixteen hour shifts while you have a newborn up in the day care? You'd drive yourself crazy wondering if it was okay. You wouldn't be able to focus."

"I wouldn't bring a baby to work, Oliver."

"Ha!"

"Why *ha*?"

"Because that means you honestly think you'd be able to leave your brand new baby at home with its father while you're out at work all day, and that's—that's—"

"That's what, Oliver?" My skin is prickling all over. I can feel my anger levels rising. I don't like the tone of his voice, or the look of contempt that's stamped itself all over him.

Oliver lets out an exasperated breath. "You can't tell me you think Zeth is stay-at-home dad material, Sloane. He wouldn't have the first clue how to care for a child. I know I haven't exactly been the guy's number one cheerleader since you started seeing him, but this has nothing to do with that. It takes a certain kind of guy to stay home and care for their kid while their girlfriend or wife goes out to work. I know I sure as hell couldn't do it. What makes you think a man like *Zeth* could? He's hardly the kind, caring, compassionate type."

"Fuck you, Oliver." I snatch up my jacket, angrily shoving my arms into it and pulling it on. "I didn't come to you so you could judge, okay? I came to you because you're my friend, and I thought you'd do your job as a doctor and be impartial."

"I can't be fucking impartial, Sloane. Of course I can't be. I *am* your friend, and as your friend I'm telling you a hard truth because I think you need to hear it. I think you know all of this already, that having a baby now will kill your career, that Zeth isn't ever going to win any father of the year awards, and you came to me exactly because you knew I wouldn't pull any punches."

"That's not true." I can't come up with anything further to say, because I'm so close to tears my throat is closing up. Also, a part of me knows he's right. A part of me did want to come here and hear him say all of this to me, so I could nod my head in agreement and resign myself to the fact that having a baby right now is the worst thing I could possibly do.

Oliver's anger softens as he watches me struggle not to break down into tears. He comes and sits beside me on the gurney, placing his hand lightly on top of mine. "Look. I don't want to be a jackass, okay. I don't want you thinking I don't have your back, because I do. Always. If you want to have this baby, and you want to carry on working, whatever, you know I'll support you. I'll do anything and everything I can to make life easy for you. I'll change diapers. I'll bottle feed. I'll be the best honorary uncle this kid has ever had. I even swear I won't say a word about Zeth ever again. I'll do all of that for you, Sloane, I promise. If that's what you want, then you got it. But the thing is…" His eyes are fixed and locked on his shoes. The strip lights overhead reflect in the polished oxblood leather, shining brilliantly. "I don't think that *is* what you want, and I think you feel terrible about it. But you have to know that doing what's right for you is never wrong, okay? It's sometimes the best thing you can do. Either way, like I said, I'm here. It's your call. Now all you have to do is make up your mind."

••••

"Zeth?" My voice rings hollow inside the vast, open space of the gym. It's dark outside, and the dim lights, suspended high above the cast concrete floor, cast just enough light to throw weird, stretched, eerie shadows from the equipment. Zeth's office door is closed, which generally means he's out, though the shutters are still up and a radio is playing quietly somewhere, which means someone has to be here. I find Michael in a small weights

183

room off the main area of the gym, sweating profusely as he works out. He smiles when he sees me.

"Come to challenge me to a few rounds in the cage, Dr. Romera?" He winks. "Zeth's already gone home. I'm assuming you're looking for him and not me?"

"Yeah, just thought I'd see if he was still here. Never mind. I'll head back and catch him at home."

"Is everything okay? You look a little…" Poor Michael. He doesn't want to be impolite; it's pretty obvious that I'm under the weather, though.

"Frazzled?" I offer, trying to help him out. "Yeah, been a rough few weeks. I'll be okay, though. I probably just need a good night's sleep."

Michael gets up and loops a towel around the back of his neck, using it to mop up the beads of sweat rolling over his shoulders and down his arms. His muscle shirt is soaked through, clinging to his stomach, displaying the wall of abs he has under there. It's weird—ever since I got with Zeth, I haven't checked another guy out. Not once. I'm not blind, though. I can see that Michael's beyond hot. With that beautiful, warm skin tone of his and those shockingly bright blue eyes, he's quite startling to look at.

"You know, when you spend as much time with someone as I have spent with Zeth, you come to know them pretty damn well," he says, cracking open a bottle of water. "And I know you love him, Sloane. I know you'd do anything for him. But you need to learn to trust him."

"I'm sorry?" His words are out of the blue, but he has this look on his face that makes me think he *knows*. He can't, though. There's just no way he possibly can. He smiles sadly.

"You've trusted him to save your life more than once, girl. And believe it or not, he's trusted you to save his a couple of times, too. I never thought I'd see *that* day. But now you have to trust him to have your back, Doc. Seems like it should be easier than everything else you've gone through, I know, but I get it. Sometimes it's hard to make a leap of faith. To count on someone. It's all too easy to assume how a person is going to react to something, but sometimes the reality will surprise you. Let him surprise you, Sloane."

I puff out my cheeks. My eyes are welling up, my palms sweating. I have no clue what I'm supposed to say to any of this. I don't know how to react. Eventually I say, "I trust him. Of course I do." I laugh. My voice is shaky as all hell. "And, boy, you don't need to talk to me about Zeth surprising me. He surprises me every day."

Michael drains the bottle of water he's holding. He crushes it in his hand, and then tosses it across the room into the trashcan. Getting to his feet, he does something very strange then. He takes a few steps, closing the space between us, and he wraps his arms around me, drawing me into a tight hug. It's so unexpected that I don't know what to do at first. I stand there, my hands pressing against the sides of my body, my eyes still stinging as he holds onto me. After a moment, I let myself go and hug him back. It feels like a relief. It feels like I'm allowing the situation to wash over me instead of trying so damned hard to hold it at bay. I close my eyes and I cry. Michael doesn't say a word about the fact that I'm sniffling like a baby into his sweat-covered shirt. He just rubs his hand up and down my back, remaining silent, which is exactly what I need.

It feels like we stand like this for a long time.

"Lacey was like a sister to me, Sloane. She was family. You took care of her and you cared for her like she was your own, too. So whatever happens in this life, know I'll be here for you, Doc. Never forget that."

SEVENTEEN

Mason

"You're fucking kidding me? Dude, three seconds ago, you were telling me there was no way you could go to LA. Now you're saying you can?" Ben's wearing nothing but his boxers and some smeared hot pink lipstick on his stomach. I dread to think where else he might have been painted pink. His apartment smells like sex, which is to say it smells like Ben's been locked up in here for the past three days, not answering his phone, not cracking a damn window for fresh air, while he goes at it with an array of morally challenged women.

I step over an up-ended carton of Chinese food, trying not to breathe in through my nose. The guy is a fucking animal. "I'm not saying I can go. I'm telling you that you *have* to go. You're such a fucking idiot, Ben. You know the guys from French's are looking for you, right? Don't you read your text messages?"

"Oh, I read them all right. Dude, you are panicking over nothing. Johnny's not pissed. Fighters pull this shit all the time. There's no way they're gonna single me out for a beating."

"They tried to kill Jameson Rayne, man. He's their prize fucking fighter. If they're okay with killing him, they're not gonna think twice about killing you."

Ben makes a disbelieving sound, waving one hand at me as he sifts through the piles of dirty cups and dishes on his kitchen counter with the other. "That's just people talking shit, Mase. They'd never tackle Rayne. You want some coffee?"

"No, I do not want some coffee. I want you to listen to me. Rayne's sister told me a bunch of heavies showed up at her place with serious designs on hurting him. They trashed her apartment, destroyed the place. She wasn't lying. Why the fuck would she?"

Ben ceases his mission for a clean coffee cup. He looks at me with narrowed eyes. Finally, a faint look of apprehension is forming on his features. "His sister told you that?"

"She did. And she said they were looking for you next. Hasn't anybody been over here looking for you?"

"Maybe once or twice. I've been pretty drunk. And busy. Very, *very* busy. I didn't exactly want to be disturbed."

Fuck. I'm surprised they didn't kick his damn door

down. I place a hand on Ben's bare shoulder, trying not to think about the last time he showered and how long ago that probably was. "I have a million fires to put out right now, B. I do not have time to stand here debating whether you're about to get murdered and chopped into little pieces by some very angry men, because I have a bunch of guys who want to chop me into little pieces, too. So can you please just find a bag, pack some shit into it, and let me drive you to the goddamn airport?"

Mac's in the hospital. I called earlier, pretending to be his son, and the nurse on duty at the desk told me he's unconscious at the moment, but that the doctors think he has a good chance of recovering. As long as the fucker's out cold, I'm okay. He can't order his guys, the guys I used to work with, to come find me and tear me to shreds. This is the only reason I'm here, dealing with Ben, instead of dealing with my own problems. I'll have to face them sooner or later, but for the moment getting my friend out of dodge is my only priority.

Ben looks blankly around his apartment, like he's at a loss for words. "I thought I was gonna have a little bit more time to make this transition, Mase. I mean, I need to tell my landlord—"

"Trust me, your landlord isn't gonna give a shit about you breaking your lease. I'll make sure your stuff goes into storage. But you gotta go. *Now*."

So he packs a bag. He throws clothes and fight gear into the biggest duffel he can find, and then he opens up a coffee jar on top of his busted up TV and takes out a huge wad of cash. Must be his earnings from the fight with Rayne. That goes into the bag, too.

We don't speak as I drive us to the airport. There's nothing left to say. He's been my friend for so long. We'll still be friends in many years, I'm sure. I'm itching to tell him all about Mac. About Lowell. About Zeth. I wish I could spill everything, every single last gory detail, but if I do that the bastard won't be going anywhere, he'll insist on staying so he can help me iron out this entire mess. That won't be a help to anyone. It'll only make things even more complicated.

It's surprisingly easy to get Ben on a flight. I hug him goodbye, begging him to keep his head down for a while, and he swears he will. I know the man, though. It's almost impossible for him to keep his head down. He'll be getting himself into all sorts of shit in California as soon as the plane's wheels touch down. Fingers crossed he knows better than to get involved with anything as stupid as match fixing out there. As he jogs up the stairs and disappears through the entrance to security, a bolt of jealousy hits me. If I didn't have Millie to care for, it would be all too easy to disappear through those gates with Ben and never come back to Seattle again. I've never resented my lot in life—even now I don't—but sometimes it's real fucking nice to imagine what could be. To be free. To be reckless. To act like a stupid kid sometimes and please myself.

These thoughts are still running through my mind thirty minutes later, when I shoot a text to Kaya, thanking her for the heads up and letting her know that Ben is long gone. She replies almost immediately.

Kaya: Come over. You can thank me in person.

It's late. Wanda's got Millie—I've been checking every hour on the hour to make sure she's okay, and apparently she's been sleeping a lot. That's a good sign. Means she's recharging her batteries. I make a quick call to check in on her again—she's just fine—and then I make another call to the hospital. Mac's still unconscious. They're a little more concerned about him this time; he should have woken up by now. They're planning on taking him for a second CT scan to check if his brain is swelling. This news doesn't hit me as hard as it should. I put Mac in the hospital after all. I'm responsible for the fact that it sounds like he might not be waking up any time soon. I can't bring myself to feel bad, though. The guy's a total psychopath, and there's no doubting his intentions for me this morning. He wasn't going to give me a stern talking to and send me on my way. He was planning on something a little more permanent, and I reacted in kind.

Kill or be killed. That's how life is going to be from here on out.

The weight of the day sits heavy on my shoulders. Going to see Kaya probably isn't the smartest thing I can do right now, but smart went out the window a long time ago, and I kind of need this. I need to be a young, reckless guy. I need to go and kiss the girl I like, and I need to forget, just for a second, about the fact that my life has turned to shit.

I text Kaya and get her address. She replies with nothing but the details I need to get to her, which makes me think she's not all that surprised that I'm coming over. She's a persistent kind of chick. I've given her no reason to believe that anything's gonna happen with us, and yet she's always seemed quietly confident that something eventually will.

I can't get the image of her sucking on that red vine out of my head. I'm thinking about that way too much as I hurry across Eastlake. My dick is already hard when I pull up outside the apartment complex. I know immediately which her place is from the boarded up window on the second floor—obviously the window Jameson launched the guy out of. Oh, shit. *Jameson*. Kaya lives with her brother, and I'm about to go up there and make out with her? With a fucking hard on poking out of my waistband? What the hell is wrong with me?

I ain't going anywhere until my dick starts to behave itself. If some dude I'd seen fighting at La Maison markets showed up at my front door, sporting an erection the size of the Fort Lewis's flagpole, and he wanted to hang out with *my* sister? Doesn't even bear thinking about. I'd make him hurt so bad he'd cry for his mama and never show his face around my sister again.

I close my eyes and think of Denise Lowell. When I first met the woman, I thought she was hot. Her body is rockin' and all of that blonde hair makes her look like she could be on the cover of Sports Illustrated or some shit. After spending five minutes with the bitch, I already hated her and couldn't wait to get the hell away, though. Now, the very thought of her coming anywhere near me is enough to make my hard-on fall flat in a matter of seconds. My dick practically shrinks up inside my body.

I banish all thought of red vines as I get out of the truck and head toward the building. I'm buzzed in without a word when I hit the call button for apartment twenty-three, and then there she is, Kaya, leaning against the peeling beige paint in the second story hallway, waiting for me. She's wearing a black sweater dress that barely covers the tops of her thighs, and a slash of bright red lipstick stains those perfect lips of hers. Her hair is ruffled all over the place, but not in an unkempt way. In an *I-paid-three-hundred-dollars-for-this-haircut* kind of way.

"You going out?" I ask. She looks like she's about to go eat at a fancy restaurant or something. I'm still dressed in the clothes I wore to work this morning, which means I'm in grease stained jeans, a washed out t-shirt and my black leather jacket. I don't look like I ought to be anywhere near her.

"No. I just got back from a date," she tells me.

I take a second to process that. A date? Is she serious? From the look on her face, she's serious. Am I supposed to react to this? I feel like I should be pissed off or something, but honestly how can I be? She's not my girlfriend. We haven't even been on a date ourselves. Regardless, the thought of her going out on a date with some other guy has my jealously levels flaring pretty high.

"It's only nine thirty," I say, making a show of checking my phone for the time. "Didn't go well?"

"It went very well, thank you. I had a nice time."

"And yet you're home, about to put your PJs on? Doesn't sound like the end of a successful date to me."

Kaya shrugs, pushing away from the wall, beckoning me to follow after her. "I'm far from putting my PJs on, Mason Reeves." She leads us along the hallway and opens a door to our right; standing to one side, she makes room for me to slip in after her. "Jameson's at work," she says. "He's probably going to be back in about a couple of hours, though. You should stick around and meet him properly. If you can withstand the grilling he'll give you as soon as he walks through the door, he might not kill you."

"That sounds promising."

"He's actually not as over protective as you might think. He normally minds his own business, lets me do

.

my thing."

"So he didn't vet the guy you just went on a date with then?"

She laughs. "You seem quite preoccupied with the fact that I just went on a date, Mason. Does it bother you?"

"Maybe a little. Shouldn't it?"

She shakes her head. "I go on lots of dates with Richard. I like talking to him. He has lots of interesting things to say."

Richard. Sounds like an old guy name. Don't meet many dudes our age with a name like Richard. "So you're dating a Dick, huh? I'm sure he's a thrill a second." I can't help but be petty. Kaya ushers me through the apartment—it's practically empty. The top of a large pine dining table is propped up against the wall beside the television, in three pieces. Fragments of a shattered chair lies on the floor next to it. It's a miracle the TV screen is in tact, given that almost every other stick of furniture in the place is damaged in some way.

"Richard's my college professor. We have dinner and like to talk once a week," Kaya says.

"Ah. You have a student/teacher relationship."

"We're physically and emotionally attracted to one another, but we only fulfill our desires to be intellectually intimate with one another."

"So you don't fuck."

Kaya smiles, her red lips upturning in a very pleasant

way that makes me think of kissing her. "No. We don't fuck."

"Why not?"

"Because it wouldn't be ethical. He's in a position of power. I'm his student. It's against the University's rules for him to physically engage with anyone he teaches."

"But you *want* to sleep with him?"

"I want to sleep with *you*, Mason. I occasionally want to sleep with other people, too. I have a high sex drive. That doesn't mean I actually do it, though."

"Maybe you should." I've always believed women should be able to sleep with whoever the fuck they want like guys do. So long as there's no cheating or underhanded sneaking around and it's all safe, a girl should be able to explore her sexuality and go on just as many adventures as guys. When I think about Kaya blowing Richard, her college professor, though, I feel more than a little unseated. Who the fuck is this guy? And what kind of electro shock device does he have strapped to his dick to stop him from trying to screw Kaya every time he lays eyes on her. I mean, her dress... *shit*. I want to rip it off her body right now with my teeth.

It's rare that she's not wearing that huge parka coat of hers. Now that I can see the delicious curves of her body, swelling in all the right places under the thin wool of her dress, I can't stop myself from imagining my hands all over her skin, cupping and squeezing tightly.

Kaya sinks gracefully down onto the couch, kicking

off the small black ankle boots she's wearing to reveal bare feet, toenails painted the same shocking red as her lips. "I think denying myself the things I want makes me appreciate them more," she says. "Sex is one of my favorite pastimes, but it wouldn't be as fun if I gave in and allowed myself to have it all the time. Would birthday cake be as special if you ate it every day instead of just once a year?"

"I don't know. I love birthday cake. I think I could eat it every day and not get sick of it." I don't mention the fact that my love for cake pales in comparison next to my love of getting my dick sucked. I can't remember the last time that happened, though. With Millie being so sick recently, and money being so tight, my life has consisted of work and hospital visits. More work, and more hospital visits.

"Trust me," Kaya says. "When you're patient, and you make yourself wait for the things you want so badly, getting them is that much more enjoyable." A seductive smile lingers on her lips. She glances down at the space next to her on the sofa. "Are you planning on standing up for the rest of the night, or d'you think you might be able to sit down. You're making me uncomfortable."

I think this is a lie. I doubt I'd ever be able to make this girl uncomfortable; she's so self-possessed and at home in her own skin. It wouldn't matter if I were standing on hot coals. Kaya would happily witness me do it and it wouldn't make her own feet itch. I sit down next to her anyway, leaving a seven-inch gap between our bodies so I'm not right on top of her. We're close enough that I can smell her, though—the warm, gentle, floral note of her perfume, and the subtle note of something rich and smoky, too.

"So your friend left town," she says. "I'm glad you managed to hunt him down."

"Yeah. Hopefully he'll be safe now that he's out of state."

"He will. Johnny and his guys are shrewd business-men, but they're not gonna waste time chasing someone halfway across the country just to teach them a lesson. They're too lazy. I keep trying to explain that to Jameson, but he's a stubborn son of a bitch. He says the only way he's leaving Seattle's in a body bag or the trunk of a car."

"He might get his wish."

"He might." She says this breezily, as if the prospect of her brother being murdered is of no consequence to her. "Like I said back at the café, though. My brother seems to have a way of always landing on his feet. He was on the roster to fight this weekend. He's still planning on showing up. I don't think Johnny's going to have him kneecapped at the last minute and make him miss his match. They'd lose too much money. Jameson's not the only person betting that he'll win, you know. Every single bookie in a twenty mile radius is betting the same way."

"I can believe it."

Kaya glances at me out of the side of her eye—a cool blue laser pointer, suddenly burning right into me. "I don't want to talk about my brother, Mason. And I'm assuming you'd rather not talk about your sister, too. What I'd really like to discuss is the matter of you fucking me, and whether you're finally going to do it tonight." She smiles sweetly.

I can't really get my head around the direct, straight-to-the-point way she says this. She must be able to tell I'm shocked even though I try and hide it, because she laughs softly down her nose. "If you're not into it, it's okay, Mase. It just seems like the next step in this particular relationship."

"But not in the *emotional* relationship you share with Richard?"

She shakes her head, trying to conceal a smile. "No, not with Richard. Would you prefer that *we* have an emotional relationship instead of a physical one?"

"You say that like the two are mutually exclusive."

"They usually are with guys. Don't you think so?"

"Maybe."

"You didn't answer my question. If you'd like to go out to dinner and discuss Proust, I'd be more than happy to split the bill with you." She scrunches up her nose, pouting those glossy lips of hers. "Personally, I think you're more of a strip down naked and fuck kind of guy, though. Correct me if I'm wrong."

My dick is harder than granite again. All she had to do

was say the words *strip down naked and fuck* and I'm ready to go. Hearing her say such things, the way she says them, is probably the hottest thing I've experienced in a long time. I shift on the couch, trying to disguise the fact that my jeans are tenting in the crotch. "You're not wrong," I tell her.

"I know. I like to study people, Mase. I like figuring them out, working out what makes them tick. You might like the idea of being emotionally involved with me, but the reality of your day-to-day life makes date night, grabbing dinner, hitting the movies, and weekends away in the mountains an impossibility. I know that. I respect that. But I still want to ride your dick."

God damn it. There's no point in pretending this isn't going to happen anymore. I came here for a reason, and Kaya knows it. I scan her features one last time, reviewing the way her Cupid's bow mouth lifts a little at the corners, the way her sharp blue eyes fizzle with an intelligence that makes me even more turned on for some reason.

"Fuck it." I grab for her, cupping the back of her neck with my right hand, and our mouths crash together as she leans in at the same time. She kisses me just as aggressively as I kiss her, our tongues both licking and teasing at each other. Jesus, she's good.

My left hand finds its way up her shirt all by itself. Kaya moans into my mouth as I cup and squeeze her breast through her bra, rolling the swollen bud of her nipple that I can feel straining against the lacy fabric. Her hands have a mind of their own, too. She takes hold of my shirt and lifts it up, pausing our kiss for a split second so she can rip it off over my head. "My god, Mason." She digs her fingernails into my chest, glancing down at my bare skin in awe. "All that fighting and working out really has paid off."

She's seen me without a shirt on at the fights many times, I'm sure. I was barely dressed when she practically blew that Red Vine at French's, sucking it into her mouth with an evil glint in her eye, fully conscious of what it would be doing to me in my head. And yet you'd think this is the first time by the way she's staring at my abs, running her slender hands up and down my body like it's something to truly be admired.

"Close your eyes," she tells me. "I want to get naked for you."

"But I'd very much like to see that," I counter.

"Just close them until everything's off. Stripping out of a tight dress is never sexy."

She's crazy if she thinks she could possibly do anything right now that would be *un*sexy, but I give her what she wants. I close my eyes shut, resisting the urge to crack my eyelids and peek. She gets up and starts rustling around, and I can feel the air moving on my skin as she throws one piece of clothing to the ground, followed by another two.

"Stay still," she says.

I feel her skin, then, touching mine. She climbs up onto me, so that she's straddling me, and places her hands over my face. "Open your eyes," she whispers.

She doesn't need to tell me twice. I'm literally speechless as I take in her naked form. She's flawless. Fucking *flawless*. She wouldn't need airbrushing if she was on the cover of a magazine. Her tits are phenomenal. They're not huge, less than a handful, but they're perky and so perfectly formed, her nipples a soft subtle color of pink that reminds me of the inside of a seashell. I place my hands on her hips, arguing with myself in my head. I want to take her. I want to pick her up and throw her down on this couch, so I can devour her piece by piece.

"You are..." *Shit*. There are no words to describe how amazing she is. I leave my mouth hanging open as I shake my head, scrambling to think of a compliment that will do her justice. It doesn't exist, though.

She blushes. Kaya Rayne has never blushed in my presence. She's always seemed too fiery and self-assured for something as girl-next-door as blushing, but the evidence is right in front of me. Her lips look swollen and plump, delectable, ready for me to bite. "Carry me to my bed, Mason?" she whispers. "I want you naked, too."

I fold her up in my arms, my brain screaming like fucking crazy when her tits press up against my chest, and I lift her from the couch. She wraps her legs around my waist tight enough that I could let go of her and she wouldn't fall; I don't let go, though. I cup my hands under her perfect ass and her perfect thighs, groaning a little when my fingers skate over her pussy and I feel wetness there.

She wants me. She wants me already, and we haven't even begun. Her body is unfamiliar and new, hiding so many secrets. I have no idea yet where she likes to be kissed, or touched, or licked, and the prospect of discovering all of those places one at a time, slowly, is beyond fucking thrilling.

In her room, I lie her down on her back, climbing up onto the mattress so I'm hovering over her. "Open your legs for me, Kaya." My voice is ragged with desire, and she reacts to the sound of it, her lips parting, a soft gasp working its way out of her. "Do it," I tell her. " I want to see. I want to see all of you."

I sit back so she can drop her knees apart, baring her pussy to me, giving me a very clear view of what I've been daydreaming about all these weeks since we met. Her pussy is the same fragile pink color as her nipples, glistening and wet. Fuck, I want to bury my face in there right now. I want to lose myself in her as I make her come with my tongue. I can almost taste her sweet, slick flesh. I can almost feel her legs tightening around my head as I bring her closer and closer, until she's tumbling over the precipice of her orgasm, screaming my fucking name.

I wait, though. Instead, I unbutton my jeans and slip

them off, kicking my shoes off and losing my socks at the same time. I stand naked in front of her, readying myself mentally for what's about to happen. I'm about to go to war.

Kaya is such as strong-willed girl. She wants what she wants, and she knows how to get it. Thing is, she's never been fucked by a guy like me before. She may have slept with strong, masculine guys, yes, but I'm betting she's had them bending over backwards, willing to snap their spines to please her in every way. I want to make her come. I want tonight to be the most mind-blowing sex of her life, but I know this experience will fade into the history of her sexual conquests, never to stand out from the rest, if I give her exactly what she wants.

She needs someone who will take her in hand. She needs someone to tell her no. And fair enough. She can tell me no, too. I'm not going to make her do anything she doesn't want to. But she's not the one in control here. Is she going to be into that? Who knows. I guess I'm about to find out, though.

"Have you watched me in the cage before, Kaya?" I ask.

She squirms a little, her hands rubbing along the lengths of her thighs. "Yes. I've seen all of your fights."

"Good. Then this will make sense to you. I fuck like I fight, Kaya. I take no prisoners. I dominate, and I take control. I hate to lose. Are you sure you still want to play with me?"

Slowly, carefully, she inches her right hand toward her pussy, until the very tips of her fingers are teasing her clit. She arches her back, her eyes still locked on mine. "I want to play. Doesn't mean I won't get my way, though, Mason. Do you want to risk losing? Just this once?"

I shake my head. Taking my dick in my hand, I squeeze, shivering a little in anticipation. Her glance flickers down, settling on the sight of my palm slowly working up and down my hard cock. I can't help but enjoy the look of expectation in her eyes. "I like taking risks," I say. "But this, in the underground fighting circuit, is what we like to call a one sided match, Kaya Rayne. Now roll over and show me that ass."

Kaya smirks. Ten seconds pass by, and I'm getting ready to grab my shit and leave. If she doesn't do as I've told her, that's exactly what's going to happen, and I think she knows it. I think she can see it in my eyes. At the eleventh second, she shrugs, propping herself up on her elbows. "Power is a dangerous thing. Make sure it doesn't go to your head, okay?"

Purposefully, slowly, she rolls herself over, kneeling a little so that her porcelain skinned ass is on display for me and me alone. Casting an amused look over her shoulder, she raises her eyebrows. "Like what you see?"

I rub my hand against the side of my leg, warming up my palm, getting ready to spank the ever-loving shit out of her. "You could say that. You could say I like what I see a lot." She gasps the first time my palm makes contact with her ass. The room fills with the sound of her surprise, which only makes me want to slap her harder. "Hold on tight, Kaya," I tell her. "You wanted this, and now you're gonna get it. I really hope you're fucking ready."

EIGHTEEN

Sloane

I lay on my side, watching him. It's late, past one in the morning, but I just can't sleep. Zeth carried me up to bed and made me lay very still while he went down on me, taking his time with his tongue. I shivered and tried to breathe slowly as he brought me to my orgasm, and when it was over he licked me clean, seeming to take great pleasure in the task. He wouldn't fuck me. Instead, he took me in his arms and stroked his hands up and down my body in the dark for an hour, tracing circles and strange, alien shapes into my skin before he eventually fell asleep.

He never gradually passes into unconsciousness. He falls dramatically, like plunging head first off a steep cliff. There's a change in him that's so instantaneous and intense that it's impossible to miss. His breathing, the tautness of his muscles, the way the air snaps with a certain energy that always rolls off him—all of that changes. His arms fall slack, his chest rising and falling slowly, rhythmically, and the sharp edge of his consciousness flees the room, leaving the space around him feeling somehow *less* because of it.

Times like these, when he's asleep, fighting dragons in his dreams, I love to watch how his face changes. He's such a hard person to know. There's a fierceness about him at all times. He loves fiercely. He fights fiercely. He exists in a way that seems like a challenge, as if he's defiant down to his very core, and no matter what, he's ready to defend his choices, his beliefs, and those he cares about regardless of what it might cost him. There's just no fear in the man.

When he's asleep, though, it's possible to catch a glimmer of softness to him if you look hard enough. The lines of his face relax. His hands, so often tightened into balls of flesh and bone, ready to attack, turn from weapons into works of art. His hands fascinate me. They're covered in scars, calloused and rough where his fingers meet his palms; a fortune teller would have a hell of a time getting a read on his future, given the way that roadmap of lines etched deeply into his skin seem so much more chaotic than most.

I wonder if I'm in there somewhere. I wonder if there's a point in the crisscross madness of those creases where one line meets another and something changes for him. Life suddenly takes on a different meaning. I know my life changed irrevocably when I met him. That change is burned deep inside my very being— in my mind, in my heart, and in my soul. Seems only fair that there should be some mark of it upon Zeth's body, too.

I press the pad of my index finger against the pad of his index finger, barely touching them together. For a moment, our fingerprints connect and it seems symbolic. We are two different people, so vastly, incomprehensibly different, and yet we are also the same because we're more than the sum of him as person, and me as a person. We're forever joined in this life. We are two sides of the same coin. Two halves of one whole. I defy anyone to tell me this isn't true.

My belly twists, a strange, slightly unsettling feeling fluttering in the pit of my stomach, and I close my eyes. It feels like the tiny life that's getting to work inside of me wants its presence to be felt right now, in this moment, while I'm musing over thoughts of Zeth and me together. Because now there is another way that we're joined, and I'm only just beginning to understand how special this new joining of our bodies and our souls actually is. A child. A baby inside me. Half of me, and half of him. God, what a complicated mess this is. Of course, it's way too soon for the baby to be moving. I won't feel him move for weeks and weeks, and yet even so, the mind is a powerful thing. It can trick you into believing all sorts of things if it wants to.

Zeth frowns, his bottom lip twitching, the dragons in his dreams giving him hell, and my heart feels like it's about to brim over. I love him so goddamn much. I never knew it would be possible to care about another person this deeply. If I give birth to this man's child, if I get to hold his son in my arms, I get the feeling I'll be dazzled by the entirely new depths of love I'll experience for the very first time. An amazing, powerful, bottomless kind of love; I see it on the faces of new mothers every day in the maternity wards.

That look is wonderful and frightening all at the same time. I'm not sure I'm prepared for it. If I could only know—

Cold blue light flashes, splitting apart the dark. The peaceful moment is shattered. My cell phone on my bedside table starts shrieking, and Zeth, lost to sleep a second ago, is upright, his eyes wide, shoulders tensed, muscles coiled, ready to explode into action. His chest is heaving, and so is mine. The surprise of the loud ringtone blaring out into the thick silence has my heart slamming like a trip hammer in my chest. Zeth's gaze locks onto me, and then he's leaning his naked body over mine, as though he's shielding me.

"You okay?" he asks. "I didn't think you were on call."

"I'm not."

He reaches over me and picks up my phone, handing it to me. I don't recognize the number on the screen. It's a local Seattle number, but not one I remember seeing before. "Sorry, I'll go take this downstairs. Go back to sleep."

Zeth wraps an arm around my waist, drawing me close to him as he lies back down in the bed. "Take it here. I don't want you going anywhere."

"Okay." I feel him kissing the back of my neck and my shoulder blades as I pick up the call. "Hello?"

"Miss Romera? Doctor Romera? Have I got the right number?" The woman on the end of the phone is breathing hard, panting as she tries to get her words out. "Please, dear god, tell me I dialed it right."

"Yes, this is she. Can I help you?"

"Yes, ma'am. My name is Wanda. I live next door to Mason. He gave me your business card in case anything happened with his little sister. I'm watchin' over Millie tonight, see, and she went to bed just fine a couple of hours ago. Everything seemed normal, but I heard her fall just now, and she's havin' a seizure, a bad one, an' I don't know what to do. It won't stop. Please, Miss. You gotta come. You gotta come and look at her."

"Hang up the phone and call 911 right away, Wanda. Call for an ambulance. I'll meet you at the hospital, okay?"

"You won't come here?" The poor woman sounds terrified.

"I can't treat her properly at your place, Wanda. I don't have the drugs she needs. Call 911. I'm leaving right now. I'll see you at the hospital."

I hang up, and Zeth's already swinging out of bed. He rifles in the chest of drawers, tugging out clothes. "I'll drive you," he tells me, as he pulls on underwear, a t-shirt and jeans.

"It's Millie, Mason's little sister. Can you see if you can find him?"

"Sure." He texts something quickly as I get dressed and rush downstairs. His phone chimes as we're hurrying out of the house. "Mason's not picking up. Michael's gonna hunt him down. He'll find him and bring him to the hospital."

Zeth drives down the mountain like a maniac. Thank god he does. I would never have the courage to speed so fast through the corners and take the hairpin bends at such a crazy clip, but Zeth's an expert driver. He's been involved in enough car chases by now that he could probably make killer money as a rally driver. Once we hit the city, things have to slow down a bit, but he knows the quickest route to St. Peter's and he doesn't take any prisoners as he ducks and weaves past the other cars still on the roads.

He pulls up outside the emergency entrance to the building and lets me out, then screeches off, tires smoking as he goes to find somewhere to park.

"Dr. Romera? What the hell are you doing here? I thought you were off sick?" The young nurse at the desk seems confused.

"Millie Reeves? Has she been brought in yet?" It's been twenty minutes at least; the ambulance should have arrived and brought her in by now. The nurse—I'm pretty sure her name is Anderson—checks the iPad screen in front of her, frowning.

"Reeves, Reeves, Reeves. Ah, yes, a second ambulance had to be sent to the scene. They should be arriving any moment."

"A *second* ambulance? What the hell happened to the first one?"

Anderson shrugs. "Some kind of engine trouble. I'm not sure."

Ambulances are checked and maintained every day. There's no way a vehicle should have broken down. Something like this could mean the difference between a patient living and a patient dying. I'm filled with dread. If the EMTs didn't get to Millie on time, she could easily slip into a coma and die.

"*Shit.*" I leave the front desk, and I run to the closest supply closet, grabbing a set of scrubs. No one says anything further about me not being on shift. I shouldn't be treating anyone right now. I'm not allowed to storm into the hospital, get changed, and then start messing with patients; that's not how the system works. Chief Allison isn't in the building, though, and I must look frantic and harried because the nursing staff and other doctors keep any objections they might have to themselves.

The ambo still hasn't arrived by the time I've changed and gone outside to wait for Millie. Damn it, this is taking too long. Zeth appears by my side. "Michael's still looking," he says. The crash team waiting on the ambulance cut wary sideways glances at the huge, tattooed guy now waiting with us. I forget how imposing he must look to people when he first meets them.

"Okay. Fuck, I hope he gets here soon. She's going to need him."

"She's got you," he says. "That's more than enough."

Lights and sirens, then. An ambulance screeching into the car park, hurtling towards us at seventy miles an hour. The driver slams on the brakes just in time, bringing the vehicle to an abrupt stop less than a meter from the hospital entrance. Chaos ensues.

The EMTs jump from the van, shouting out Millie's stats. Her tiny body is transported out of the ambulance and rushed inside. I run with the crash team, taking in everything the EMT is shouting: erratic pulse. Pupils fixed and dilated. At least seventeen minutes of continuous convulsions in the field. Famipentol administered, to no effect. Maximum dosage limit reached.

The famipentol should have knocked the seizure on the head. Millie should be awake by now. We can't give her any more. If we do, not only could it cause severe damage to her internal organs, but it could also send her into coronary failure as well. It can't be risked.

"Push sodium valproate. Someone page neuro, tell

them what's going on. We need a consult right away." An intern, one I don't recognize, takes off down the hall, sneakers squeaking on the linoleum as he skids and disappears around a corner, on the hunt for a phone.

We take Millie into a procedure room. Standard protocol is observed. Millie's hooked up to a heart monitor. Her levels are recorded. I have a nurse push clobazam, but that doesn't seem to have any effect, either. Millie remains on her back on the gurney, the heels of her feet hammering against the padding and the sheet, head tipped back, jaw locked, eyes rolled up into the back of her head. She's in trouble. Big, big trouble. God, she looks so tiny and helpless as the seizure continues to contort her fragile little body. This episode has already lasted too long. Wanda called me forty minutes ago at least, and for a six-year-old to be seizing like this for such a long time? I don't want to think about what it means. I can't even think about it, because if I do I'll have to admit the truth: that I know all hope is lost.

Dr. Mike Margate, head of neurology, shows up almost immediately. He assesses Millie, his movements confident, however the look on his face is far from it. "Left pupil's blown now," he says. "Could be an early sign of brain herniation. We're not going to know what's going on in there until we give her a scan, but we can't keep her still for that."

Dr. Hamid, a new member of the intern's program, looks wrecked by this news. "What about sedation?

Can't we knock her out?" he asks.

Margate sends a glance my way. "Dr. Romera? Care to explain to Dr. Hamid why sedation is a bad idea in this case?"

"She's already had everything we can give her. Her system's flooded. If we sedate her, it's going to be too much for her body to take. Her respiratory system will fail."

"Exactly." Margate runs a small wooden paddle up the sole of Millie's right foot, waiting to see if her body responds in anyway. It's difficult to tell if there's any natural reaction, since her body is still shaking so violently. He frowns then, bending down, peering closely at the side of Millie's ankle. "When did this show up?" he asks. "Does she have any other marks on her body?"

It takes me a second to see what he's pointing to: a tiny red mark on the inside of her leg, just above her ankle. It looks like a rash, though the mark appears to be on its own. Hands are on Millie, then. Four people quickly cut her pajamas from her body, leaving scraps of the Power Puff Girls printed fabric scattered on the floor. Everyone pores over Millie's tiny frame, scanning for more red marks.

I see one low on her ribcage, again all by itself. "There. *Shit.*"

An intern raises his hand, a wary look on his face. "Does this mean…does this mean bacterial meningitis?"

Margate shakes his head. "Not bacterial. Check her

charts. Is she on Lamictal?"

I already know that she is. "Yes," I answer. "For sixteen months."

"Then that's it, people. Things just got officially worse. She's probably got aseptic meningitis. Let's get her under right away. We're gonna have to roll the dice on this one after all, I'm afraid. We'll only be able to fight the swelling in her brain if she's unconscious. She's going to have to be monitored around the clock, though. "You," he says, pointing at an intern. "Do not leave this child's side."

"But my shift's up in thirty—" He stops talking when Margate looks up at him, pinning him with a look of fury. "Yes, sir. Of course. I won't leave her."

"Good. Get that scan immediately, people. I want to see what's going on inside that head of hers."

Margate leaves. Millie's still shaking on the gurney. We won't be able to get her sedated quick enough. Her body needs a break from the constant beating its taking. When I look up, about to start ordering people into action, I notice Zeth standing in the doorway of the procedure room. He's leaning against the doorframe, arms folded across his chest, and his expression is dark to say the least.

We'd never normally allow a civilian to observe like that, but he's not your average civilian. He wasn't panicking like most people would have been. He didn't say a word. He kept his mouth shut and he watched, by the looks of things, and he didn't interfere. Margate didn't even remark on his presence as he left the room, which means he probably thought Zeth was another doctor or something.

I take hold of him by the arm as the nurses wheel Millie out and up the corridor toward the elevators, where they'll then take her for an MRI. "Don't you want to go home and wait for me there? It's the middle of the night," I say.

He follows Millie with his eyes as she's taken away. "I'll wait here." His voice is flat, monotone, and cold. "*You* shouldn't even be here. You're gonna need a ride when you're done."

"Michael could always run me back later."

Zeth shakes his head. I can tell by the stoic, emotionless way he's holding himself that he won't be swayed on the matter. He doesn't blink until the elevator doors have closed and Millie's out of sight. "What's gonna happen to her?" he asks. "Best guess."

I don't want to tell him the truth, but I also don't want to lie. I hesitate, and then say, "Her outlook isn't good. She's so young. With such a violent, prolonged seizure, and the likelihood that she's developed aseptic meningitis, chances are she'll either...just stop breathing when we put her under, or her brain will have swollen to the point where there's nothing we can do for her." It feels like bad luck to paint such a grim picture of the next twelve hours, but trying to create a different image altogether will only serve to get my own hopes up, and that's dangerous. Zeth clears his throat.

"She's so small. I didn't know his sister was so young. He's been taking care of her all by himself."

"Yeah. Since she was a baby."

Turning his back on the elevator, Zeth straightens his shoulders, inhaling deeply. "I'm not hanging around in the waiting room. I'm coming with you."

"You can't. This is a hospital, Zeth. People can't just wander around wherever they like. It'd be a madhouse."

"Are you going to report me to security?" he asks, lifting an eyebrow.

"No, of course not. But—"

"All right. Well until someone says something, I'm with you. The moment I'm asked to leave, I'll go. Until then, I'm your fucking shadow."

There's nothing I can say that will change his mind now. I've learned to pick my battles with this man. If letting him observe what happens with Millie means I'll be able to claim a victory for myself at some other time, then so be it. "Urgh. Fine. But you're going to need scrubs or something."

Zeth, for a fleeting second, looks charmed by the idea of scrubs. I find him a clean set in the residents' lounge, and he quickly strips down and puts them on. Upstairs on the neuro ward, Millie's already been put under. Only the soles of her bare feet are visible from inside the MRI machine. I leave Zeth in the control booth with a very frightened looking resident at the computer, observing the scan as it progresses, and I head out to find Margate. I need to know what he's thinking—if there's anything further that can be done while we're waiting for the results of the MRI to be compiled. I'm halfway down the hall when an alarm starts wailing and the door to the MRI room flies open. The resident who was studiously fixated on the stills flashing up on the screen in front of him, doing his best to ignore Zeth a moment ago, is now racing toward me, face white as a freshly starched sheet.

"She's coding. She's fucking coding," he gasps.

We run.

Thankfully the resident's turned the MRI off. We slide Millie out of the narrow tube, and she is still, and cold, and worryingly blue. "She's not breathing. Arrhythmic tachycardia. Fuck. Her heart's giving out. Go get the paddles."

The resident does as I command. A second later, I have defibrillator paddles in my hands and Millie's hospital gown is open, exposing her pale, almost translucent skin. The intern Margate told not to leave Millie's side hugs the wall by the door, watching with terror in his eyes.

The defibrillator makes a high-pitched whining noise and then an alarm sounds, signaling that it's charged. "Clear!"

The resident throws his hands up. I plant the paddles on Millie's little chest, and I administer the charge. Her body jumps, her muscles tautening and releasing in quick succession. The heart rate monitor beside the gurney continues to shriek, the peaks and troughs of Millie's heart beat spiking erratically. It didn't work. Damn it, it didn't work.

"Still arrhythmic. Charge again." I won't stop until she stabilizes.

The defib whines. I call clear. I shock her again.

Still nothing.

I do it again. I increase the voltage beyond what is safely recommended for the body of a little child. I feel like I'm swimming under water, not breathing, dying for oxygen, and yet I know I can't come up for air until I save the little girl in front of me.

Still, nothing.

"Dr. Romera, we have flat line."

"Charge to five hundred. Clear."

"Dr. Romera—"

"I said charge to five hundred!" I can hear the monotone pitch of the flat line alarm on the heart rate monitor, but I refuse to accept it. I refuse to acknowledge it. I know all too well that the defib won't work if Millie has no pulse at all—how can it regulate her pulse if there isn't one to begin with?—but I can't give up now.

The resident standing by the defib looks uncertain. He must read the desperation in my eyes, though, because he does as I tell him to and he punches in the new voltage.

I shock Millie. Her head bounces on the gurney, her blue lips parting slightly, the tips of her tiny teeth showing, and still the heart rate monitor remains the same.

"Flat line, Dr. Romera. No pulse."

I throw down the paddles and link my hands together, starting compressions on Millie's chest. *One, two, three, four, five, six, seven,...* I count to thirty, and then I start counting all over again.

Fuck.

At some point I feel a sickly crunching beneath my hands: I've broken Millie's ribs. I pause, barking at the resident. "Check for a pulse!"

He does. His eyes tell me what I need to know. Again, I start compressions.

"Dr. Romera, she's gone. You should...you should probably stop now."

Someone's hand is on my arm. I rip it off, growling under my breath. "Step back. Step back *right now*."

...*sixteen, seventeen, eighteen, nineteen, twenty*... All the way to thirty again. I lean back, hands raised up by my head. "Check for a pulse." The resident heaves a deep breath, shaking his head. He presses his fingers into Millie's neck, eyes on the heart rate monitor, which is still reporting a flat line, and he sighs.

"Still nothing. She's gone, Dr. Romera. We need to—"

I ignore him. I link my hands together again and I get to work. Everything becomes hazy. I know I ask for the resident to check her pulse one more time, but I don't hear his response. I focus on pumping Millie's chest up and down, pushing her blood around her body. Her cells need oxygen. Her brain needs a continuous blood supply. When Margate gets here, he'll be able to do something. He'll fix it. He'll—

"*Sloane.*"

The sound of that voice cuts through the spiraling madness taking over my mind. I look up from Millie's rapidly cooling body to find Zeth standing in the doorway of the MRI suite. His eyes are pinned on me, solid and grounding. "You need to stop now," he says quietly. His voice is low, but it contains a commanding timbre that halts me dead in my tracks. "There's nothing more you can do," he tells me. "It's done. It's over now. It's time to stop."

A deep, unwavering pain settles on my chest, making it hard to breathe. "But—she's only six," I whisper. "She's only a *baby.*"

They say all doctors get one. You can go through your entire career as a medical practitioner, treating your patients with the cool, calm reserve you need to be good at your job, and then one day, out of the blue, you'll lose someone and it will feel like that loss will kill *you*. I've never broken down over a dying patient before. My hands have been steady, no matter what. Today, all of that changes. Poor little Millie, so young and so full of life, is my *one*. The one that will break me. My legs feel like they're about to go out from underneath me.

"What am I going to—what am I going to tell Mason?" Tears streak down my face. God, this isn't how a senior resident is supposed to conduct themselves in front of their subordinates. I can't seem to get a handle on myself, though.

"You tell him you did everything you could," Zeth says. "Because you did. I saw it all. It was an impossible situation, Sloane." He enters the room, glaring at the resident and the intern. "Leave," he growls. "Go get someone or something."

Both of them scurry out of the room. Zeth scoops me up into his arms and holds me against his body; I collapse, his heat and the security of his strong arms around me keeping me safe. I allow myself another moment of weakness, and I sob. She's gone. I can't believe it happened so quickly. We didn't even get chance to assess her properly. The strain on her body was obviously too much.

"You're a wonder," Zeth whispers into my hair. "You're amazing. You fought so hard."

"Not hard enough." I feel as though I failed. It's normal for a doctor to feel that way, they tell us. That we'll feel like we've let the ones who lose down. I know the truth: Millie was very sick. She was beyond saving. But at the same time, I can't help but feel like she placed her trust in me to keep her safe, and that trust was misplaced.

"Don't." Zeth kisses my temple, his breath blowing hot against the side of my face. "You're not god. You can only do so much."

He's right. It still hurts, though. It still hurts more than any pain I've ever felt. "You need to go," I whisper. "They'll be here for her body in a moment. You can't be here when they come."

"Okay. I'll check on Michael, see if he's managed to locate Mason yet." He leaves, and I'm left alone with the little girl on the table. She looks so small. So fragile. She looks like she's sleeping.

Above her on the wall, I check the plain white clock, its hands slowly ticking by the minutes, oblivious of the tragedy that has just occurred. My voice is nothing more than a whisper, and yet it feels as though I'm shouting.

"*Time of death, one thirty-six am.*"

NINETEEN

Sloane

I wake up to thumping. Sunlight's pouring in through the gauzy, thin, frankly pointless material that hangs over the windows next to the bed I find myself in. *Kaya's bed.* Somewhere I can hear someone shouting. Movement behind me. Kaya throwing an arm over me, her hand landing lightly on top of my bare stomach.

"Oh my god. I will pay you a million dollars to go see who that is," she groans.

"No way. What if it's your brother?"

"My brother came home at four am. He has a key, remember?"

Great. So I'm going to be sneaking out of Kaya's bedroom in my underwear at...at *six am* in the morning? *Shit.* Wanda normally brings Millie back to the apartment at seven when she sleeps over. I have one hour to get home and showered before she shows up, otherwise I am in the shit.

"*Mason! Mason, open the fucking door!*" Three loud bangs echo through the apartment. I am suddenly very, *very* awake. Whoever's out there knows my fucking name. Is it one of Mac's boys? Did the fucker finally wake up and order my death warrant. Where the hell is my phone? I need to get the fuck out of here. This place had better have a fire escape.

"Who did you tell that you were coming here?" Kaya asks blearily.

"No one. I told no one." I scramble out of bed, searching for my boxers, which are proving hard to locate. I find them kicked under the bed, along with a balled up wad of denim that turns out to be my jeans. I get dressed in a hurry, grabbing my shirt from the lounge. My cell phone is sitting on the coffee table, dead—it goes into my back pocket. I hear the front door opening, and then a deep voice echoing down the hallway.

"Mason doesn't live here. If you don't stop hammering on this door, I'm gonna knock your fucking teeth down your throat, asshole."

"Is that so?" I recognize the voice. Takes a moment to place it, and then it hits me; it's not one of Mac's guys, it's one of Zeth's. It's Michael.

I duck into the hallway, mostly dressed now but missing socks and shoes. Jameson stands by the front door, looking like he's about to launch himself at the tall, well-dressed guy standing in front of him. Michael sees me and jerks his head back behind him. "Come on. We have to go."

Jameson does a double take. "What the fuck? Where did *you* come from?"

"I'll let your sister explain." Snatching up my shoes, I slip past him out into the corridor.

"*Kaya*!" Jameson does not sound too happy. I don't hang around to find out what he thinks about me spending the night with her; it can only lead to trouble. I'm sure Michael's presence signifies more of the same, but I doubt he's going to try and tear me limb from limb. At least I hope he's not.

He grabs me by the shirt and begins to drag me down the hall. "Why the fuck haven't you been answering your phone, you idiot?" he snaps.

"The battery died. What...Jesus, *tell me what the hell is going on*!" I wrestle myself free, hurrying after him.

"We need to get to the hospital. *Now*."

The hairs on my arms stand up. My legs are lead weights. I can't move another step. Oh god. God, no. I grind to a halt, my tongue nothing more than a thick piece of meat in my mouth. "It's not Mac, is it?" I say softly.

Michael turns to face me. His ghostly pale blue eyes are full of bad news. "No. It's not Mac."

Sloane

The morgue seems especially quiet. Bochowitz has done his work, cleaning and preparing Millie's body. There's no need for an autopsy. The majority of Millie's MRI scan was completed before she coded, and it showed a devastating amount of swelling to her brain. It would have killed her no matter what. The combination of drugs in her system, along with the strain on her heart, managed to kill her first though. Both Margate and myself signed off on the cause of death, which means Millie's body won't need to be cut open and investigated—a small blessing.

Bochowitz left the morgue after his work was done—said he couldn't bear to see Millie all laid up and silent after spending so much time with her here before, when she was very much alive and full of laughter. That has left Zeth and I standing vigil over her body, while we wait.

To one side, I see something familiar and shiny sitting on a metal tray. The personal affects of the deceased are usually set to one side like this, ready for family members to claim, and Millie is no different. Except this time, there aren't a handful of belongings quarantined, awaiting collection: wallet, phone, wedding rings, bunches of keys. There is only a scuffed imitation Rolex watch—*my* scuffed imitation Rolex watch. She must have been wearing it when they brought her in. I didn't notice. I didn't see. My heart throbs fitfully once more, aching without end. Slowly, I collect the watch. I don't need it anymore. It's Millie's. I unclip the strap and thread it over her tiny hand, fastening it as tightly as I can. Her wrist looks so narrow and slender, so goddamn small. I feel like bursting into tears, but I don't.

Hours pass by. After a long time, Zeth sits himself up on the edge of the cold metal slab Millie is laid out on, where he takes hold of her and lifts her into his arms. He folds the sheet covering her body around her, wrapping her up as if to keep her warm, and he just sits like that, stroking her hair, rocking her in his arms. He doesn't say a word.

I try really fucking hard, but I can't keep my tears at bay. Always, Zeth has seemed like an impenetrable brick wall. The weather and the tides crash against him and have no effect. All hell breaks loose, and he stands strong, unharmed. He holds this little girl in his arms now, though—a little girl he had never met before tonight—and he seems completely undone.

Those huge hands of his move slowly over Millie's fine, wispy hair, and after a while I can hear the deep, low rumble of his voice as he whispers softly to her. It's a tender, painful thing to watch. I can't hear what he says to her, and I don't want to, either. That's between him and Millie.

Another hour passes.

Zeth's phone starts ringing in his pocket, but he

doesn't answer. Neither of us move to leave, because it doesn't seem right somehow. Millie shouldn't be left alone. Eventually, the door to the morgue opens and Michael slips inside. His shoulders are stiff, lines deeply creasing his forehead as he takes in Zeth rocking Millie in his arms.

"*God*," is all he can say. He rubs one hand over his face, placing the other one on his hip. "I found him. He's outside. I didn't know if I should bring him in or not."

I get to my feet, wincing when my hips and back complain. I've been sitting for too long. "Okay. Does he know?"

Michael winces, too, though I think it's his heart that's hurting him. "I think so. I didn't have to tell him. He followed me down here without saying a word. It's like his body's out there but his mind is somewhere else completely."

So he does know, then. He's figured it out, and now he's in shock. I'd like to think that means I don't have to go out there and tell him his little sister is dead, but being informed is part of the process. He needs to hear me say it. I really don't want to. It's going to destroy me to part with the words, but no matter how badly it will hurt me, it's going to hurt him a million times more. He's cared for Millie for so long. She's been his sole responsibility, the only real thing he's had to care about in the whole world, and now she's gone.

I move out into the corridor in silence, closing the

door behind me as quietly as I can. Mason is sitting on one of the plastic chairs opposite the entrance to the morgue, staring into space. I take a seat next to him, trying to pull in a deep breath without being too obvious.

"Mason—"

"I've never chased girls, y'know," he says evenly. "I was really fucking young when I had to take Millie on, and all I wanted to do was drink and fight and fuck. I knew I couldn't do that if I was going to be a solid figure in her life, though. I quit drinking so much. I never went out. I forgot all about dating and finding myself a girlfriend. I mean, what girl would have wanted to date a guy with a little kid hanging off his hip all the time?" He lets out a shallow huff, meant to be laughter. "I got through the last year of high school. I got a job. I worked for fucking years, keeping my head down, and then the one night...the *one* night I fuck up...*that's* the one night she needs me. *That's* the one night I'm nowhere to be found."

"Mason, she didn't know you weren't here. She was unconscious the whole time." This is such a useless, worthless thing to tell him. It's not going to make him feel any better and I know it. I hate myself for even saying it, but he needs to know.

He makes a strangled, choking sound at the back of his throat. "When did she die? What time? Exactly?"

"Around one thirty."

"It's nearly seven now. That means she's been gone for six whole fucking hours, and I was...I was asleep, in bed with some girl, and she's been here, alone." His voice cracks and breaks, choked with emotion. He tries to say something else, but instead he bursts into tears, leaning forward, elbows propped on his knees, face buried in his hands.

"She was alone. She was fucking alone," he sobs.

"She wasn't, Mason. We were here with her. We didn't leave her for a second, I swear. We were here. We were here." I repeat it over and over again, rubbing my hand up and down his back. I'm crying myself, unable to prevent a sea of tears from spilling down my cheeks. "Zeth's inside with her now. And Michael," I tell him.

"Zeth?" Mason looks sideways at me, confusion all over his face. His eyes are brimming over, his cheeks mottled and red. He is the vision of a broken man. "Zeth came?" he asks.

I nod. Who knows how Mason's going to feel about Zeth being here. The last time they saw each other, I was begging my boyfriend not to kill the guy. Mason wrings his hands together, his body beginning to shake. "That's nice," he says under his breath. "I suppose it's nice of him to come." I don't think he's really comprehending what he's saying right now, not really thinking about it. He seems numb, the shock hitting him in waves. Those waves won't stop. They'll keep on coming, hitting him for days. Weeks, even. Months. They'll still be washing over him years from now, when he least expects them, washing over him out of nowhere, causing his heart to ache in the most exquisitely painful way.

"Do you want to go and see her now?" I ask, whispering softly. "Do you want to come and say goodbye?"

He looks at me once more, eyes filled with wild panic. "I can't do that. Not yet. It's too soon."

No point in trying to rush him. I don't. I let him try to recover himself a little, but the fact of the matter is that his composure and calm will fly right out of the window as soon as he walks through that door and sees that little girl. I'll be here for him if he wants me to, but Mason is really going through this alone.

No one can feel the same pain he's feeling right now. And, no matter how badly I might want to, no one can carry it for him, either.

TWENTY

Zeth

I never knew Lacey when she was this small. I would have liked to. I would have been a grade A asshole to her when we were kids, probably, pulling on her hair and teasing the shit out of her, but I would have loved her. I would have protected her. If we'd been little together, had a childhood together, grown and formed as people together, no one would have laid a finger on her. I wouldn't have let them. She would have grown up unharmed, and she wouldn't have been so withdrawn from the world. She wouldn't be dead right now, I know that much.

"Hey, man. Maybe you should put her down now," Michael says. He's been leaning silently against the bank of silver drawers where the bodies are kept for the last fifteen minutes, watching me hold Millie. I could tell he didn't think it was a smart thing for me to be doing, but he's refrained from saying anything until now. I don't say anything. I slide off the edge of the table and I carefully place Millie back down on the bare metal. She's still covered by a sheet, but she looks uncomfortable. I find a dark blue cord jacket hanging on the back of a chair on the other side of the room and I bundle it up, tucking it under the girl's head.

One last look at her and I know I need to go.

"All right, kid. Sleep well, huh?" I stroke her hair one last time, brushing a few stray strands back behind her ear, and then we go. Out in the hallway, both Sloane and Mason startle when the door swings open. Mason, poor bastard, looks like he's about to die himself. I know exactly how he feels. When Lacey died, I couldn't even speak properly for days. I fucking hate thinking about how raw the pain was back then. It was brutal, all consuming. I thought I was never going to emerge out of the other side of it. Some days, I feel like I still haven't.

I place my hand on Mason's shoulder. "Sorry," I tell him. It's the only thing I can offer him. No platitudes or *it-will-get-better-with-time*s. Those are pointless. Sorry is the only thing that actually *means* something.

Sloane looks beaten down. She gives me a sad, tired smile, and I have to stop myself collecting her up in my arms and forcing her to come home with me. She looks like she needs sleep. She definitely shouldn't be here, but she's committed to her job. It wouldn't matter if she didn't know the guy sitting next to her from any other stranger on the street; she would stay with him and comfort him for as long as he needed her. She's not walking away from Mason any time soon.

"Call me if you need me," I tell her. She nods. Quickly, she gets to her feet and throws her arms around my neck, hugging me. I kiss her on the top of her head, and then on the mouth, deeply, trying to pass some of my strength into her. She doesn't need it; my angry girl is a badass. At a time like this, though, there's no harm in sharing a little.

Michael's on my heels as I leave the hospital. "Do you want me to follow you back? I have my Lexus here."

"No, it's fine. Go home. Sleep. You've been out all night."

"You know me. I'll sleep when I'm dead."

I slap him on the shoulder, grunting. "I'll catch you at the gym later." Fuck telling him that I need a minute to myself. Fuck telling him that seeing that little girl still and lifeless back there has hollowed me out beyond belief. He reads all of these things on me, though. He's known me long enough to be able to gauge my moods. Michael retrieves his keys from his pocket and gives me a perfunctory nod.

"Later, then."

I drive the Camaro away from St. Peter's, and with every mile I put between myself and that place I feel heavier instead of lighter. I want to smash my fists into something—heading to the gym is probably the best thing I can do for myself right now, but I find myself driving in the direction of the warehouse instead. Back to Lacey. We lived together there for a short period of time, but the open rooms, hallway and vast, empty spaces are so full of memories that it sometimes feels like she's still there somehow, crashed out on the couch, eating her breakfast cereal, watching TV.

My body is on autopilot, my brain somewhere far, far away, and so I smell the smoke before I see it. A thick, chemical tang thickens in the air as I get closer to the warehouse. Acrid and bitter, the smell grows stronger and stronger until my mind finally snaps back to reality, and I see it: the large, billowing plume of dirty black smoke funneling up toward the sky like a tornado right in the middle of the docklands.

I already know where it's coming from by the distance and the location of the smoke, and I already know what I'll see when I turn the next corner: the warehouse, burning. The warehouse on fire.

An alarm is drilling the air somewhere close by. It grows louder, piercing my eardrums, when I park up twenty feet from the burning building and climb out of the car.

What. The. Fuck?

The flames have melted the glass in the window frames on the second floor. The roller door at street level that I always keep locked is still chained, but the metal is warped and turned rust-red. It makes a wobbling, popping noise as I take a step toward the place. Inside, a loud crashing sound splits the air, as something collapses—a support beam or an internal wall.

The fire is well established. Must have been burning for some time. There are no fire trucks or police parked up out front, though. Everyone around here knows better than to call 911 in a situation like this. Who's to say what the fire fighters or the cops would find in a building like mine. No, the people on the docks are all too aware I'd skin them alive if I found out they'd placed that call, so no one has dialed, and so the building has burned.

The heat from the furnace is almost unbearable. It feels as though it will melt the skin from my bones as I get closer and closer. A huge crack, from the roof down to the very foundations of the building, has rented the main wall almost in two. Inside, every stick of furniture, every book, every single possession Lacey ever brought home with her, is being eaten by the flames.

Motherfucker.

There is absolutely no way in hell this happened on its own. Someone started this. Someone purposefully poured the gasoline and lit the match. When the fire crews eventually do show up, they'll report that this fire was the result of faulty wiring, or a leaky gas line. They won't want to involve themselves in business that doesn't concern them. They'll find it, though—the accelerant, the device, or the incendiary projectile that was used to cause this inferno—and they'll then pretend like they know nothing about it.

I know, though. I know someone has taken it upon themselves to declare war, and I have a feeling I know perfectly well who that was.

My suspicions are confirmed when I notice the chunk of metal sticking out of the roller shutter. I don't know how I missed it—the sharp wedge of steel jammed into the shutter, almost buried up to the hilt. A butcher's cleaver. The wooden handle itself is on fire, blue flames biting and licking at it. There might as well be a note attached to it, saying '*courtesy of the Barbieri family.*'

Roberto Barbieri, also known as the Butcher of Brooklyn, obviously received my gift. I had doubts Milo would survive the three-day journey back to New York with barely any food or water to keep him going. Obviously he did, though. This is the backlash. Roberto Barbieri clearly didn't like how I rearranged his boy Milo's face, or fractured his ribs, and so he has sent a little message of his own in return. This is how feuds begin. One side pokes first, and the other responds. A lifetime of tit for tat ensues, culminating in a generation of blood and death that consumes both parties.

And I'm about to jump in with both fucking feet.

You don't pitch battle against a guy like me and expect there to be no fall out. You don't come into my city and fuck with my home, and expect to sleep soundly ever a-fucking-gain. I won't tolerate it. I won't allow it. This is only the beginning. If I let this slide, Barbieri will own Seattle. He won't come here and rule it himself. He *will* send someone in his stead, and I'll forever be looking over my shoulder.

So it comes to this. A war, after all. Seattle is my home. It's where I grew up. It's where I met Sloane. I've walked these streets my entire life, and I won't give them up now. Blood will stain my hands again. Death will come circling above my head.

As I watch the hungry flames demolish what is left of the warehouse, steel hardens in my veins. Those motherfuckers will wish they'd never heard the name Zeth Mayfair. I swear, they'll wish they'd never been born.

TWENTY-ONE

Sloane

Mason weeps over his sister. It's the most awful, heartbreaking thing I've ever seen. I stay with him until he's so exhausted he can barely keep his head up, and then I drive him back to the house. He tries to put up a fight, says he ought to stay with Millie, ought to go back to his own place, but we both know he doesn't really want to be alone right now. The house is empty when we arrive. I show him where the shower is, along with the spare room, and I tell him to make himself at home. He washes up and then collapses on the bed, falling into a deep, much needed sleep. Sleep is going to be his best friend for the next few weeks. If he's asleep, it means he doesn't have to face reality. He can switch everything off. He can still dream that Millie is alive and everything is okay.

The afternoon slips away. I don't call Zeth. I saw how the events of the past twenty-four hours affected him—he needs some time to process. And so do I.

He stayed with me while I treated Millie. He refused to leave either me or her at every turn. When she died, he helped me to face the truth, and then he held her with such tenderness for hours. He brushed her hair and he rocked her, whispering to her...and I could see it. I could see the father in him.

Granted, it was a tragic situation and his actions were driven by sorrow for the young girl who lay dead in his arms, but it was there to see, plain as day—the soft, fragile, gentle, kind part of him that would make him a great father. I was scared before. Scared that the wild, dangerous parts of his life would mean he couldn't connect with anything but the savage aspect of his nature. I know now, with an unwavering certainty, that that's not the case at all.

A calm has settled over me. A heavy, relaxed state of peace. I'm not afraid at all anymore. I *know* we can do this. I know we can have this baby. It won't be easy. There will be times when I worry I've made the wrong decision, I'm sure, especially when it comes to having to take a step back from work, even if it's just for a little while, but in the long run things are going to be just fine.

Now, thank god, the panic and the fear that has been hanging over me like a dark cloud for the past few days has gone. I don't know how I would have borne it on top of the bright, stinging ache I carry in my heart for Millie and for Mason right now. It would be too, too much.

I must fall asleep. When I wake, it feels like hours have passed. Zeth's crouched by the side of my chair, and he's slowly stroking his hand up and down my arm. "Hey," he whispers. He smells strange, like burned plastic or singed hair or something. A dark, sooty line runs across his cheekbone and down, ending just above his jawbone.

"What the hell happened to you?"

"Fire. The warehouse is gone," he says. "I stood there and watched it burn until the flames went out. An empty shell...that's all that's left."

"Holy shit. Are you okay? No one was inside?"

He shakes his head. "I'm fine. No one was inside."

I just stare at him, trying to figure out what this news means. Zeth watches me with unreadable eyes, his mouth drawn into a tight line. He's furious, I can feel the anger sizzling off him, but I can't quite figure out what he's thinking. "This wasn't an accident?" I ask.

"No. The Italians."

My relief from earlier this afternoon disintegrates. This is bad news. Really fucking bad news. Why is this happening now? Of all the times for things to blow up in our faces, now is the worst possible time. Only a matter of mere hours have passed since I talked myself into thinking having a child would be an okay thing for us. More than okay; it would be a *good* thing. And now I see that familiar spark of darkness in Zeth, and everything I told myself is turning out to be a lie.

"Sloane..." Zeth takes my hand in his and brings it to his mouth, pressing the back of my hand against his lips and leaving it there. He seems to be thinking. Then, he says, "I have to go to New York."

My stomach plummets like a stone cast into deep water. "Why?"

"You know why. I can't let this go unanswered." He growls, his voice filled with fury. "If I don't do something about them setting the warehouse on fire, they're gonna set this place on fire next. Probably while we're in our fucking beds. I won't let that happen. I'm not gonna let anyone hurt you. Ever. I'll kill every single last one of those motherfuckers before they lay so much as a finger on you. That means I have to go to New York."

"Let's just leave Seattle. Let's...let's go to New Mexico. Stay with Rebel and Alexis." I'm scrambling, desperately trying to reason him out of this. He can't go to New York. If he does, he probably won't be coming back, and then what? The mafia isn't just one guy surrounded by an entourage of minions who can't think for themselves. These guys have a hierarchy. If Zeth kills the head of the family that is challenging him right now, the problem doesn't go away. Someone else picks up the reins, and they'll be seeking revenge as well as trying to assert their power. Zeth will be torn to pieces, and I'll be alone here in Seattle, stranded, maybe in danger too, and I won't have a clue how to live without him. It looks like my suggestion has pissed him off though, because his expression is stormy, his shoulders pulled back.

"I don't run from fights, Sloane. And I sure as shit don't run to Rebel. You're barely speaking to your sister. You'd fucking hate it in New Mexico."

"Not as much as I'd hate it if you were dead."

He rocks back onto his heels, his eyebrows rising slowly. "You think they'd kill me? What makes you think I wouldn't destroy all of them for what they've done?"

"You could. You might, but what if you don't? If you die, Zeth, *I die*."

This stops him in his tracks for a moment. "If they did kill me, Michael would protect you," he whispers. "You wouldn't die."

"I'd die because I wouldn't want to live anymore, you asshole! My life would be over without you in it. I couldn't—I can't even—" Tears have filled my eyes, clouding my vision. I can barely see him anymore. It's fortunate because I don't *want* to look at him. I want to screw my eyes shut and pretend this isn't happening. Not today. Not with Mason upstairs, broken and in pieces, and the rest of the world falling down around our ears.

Zeth makes a growling sound, deep in his chest. It's so deep, filled with such frustration, that I can practically feel it vibrating through the chair. "You know me, angry girl. I can't just look the other way."

"Not even for me?" His jaw is set. I can see him warring with how he is going to respond to that question. "Jesus, Zeth. *If not for me, will you do it for your unborn baby?*"

The words hit him hard, like a slap to the face. He blinks, jerking, his back ramrod straight. He holds his breath, his lips pressed tightly together. *Shit.* Shit, shit, shit. What have I done? I shouldn't have blurted it out like that. I should have told him as soon as I found out myself, I know that, but I needed the time to think. And now I just let the news burst out of me like that? It feels like time is standing still.

I can't gauge the look on his face. Is he happy? Is he angry? God, he just looks confused. He slowly rises to his feet, so that he's towering over me. "You're pregnant?" His voice is low and soft, like he's scared to form the shape of the words with his mouth, let alone allow them past his lips.

I nod.

He's not happy. I cover my face with my hands. I can't breathe. I can't fucking *breathe*. I love this man so much. He is the blood that keeps my heart pumping. The oxygen that fills my lungs. The balm that soothes my soul. If he hates me for this, if he resents me, it will shatter me into pieces.

"How?" He says the word quietly, the sound of it weighty and resonant in the still air.

I explain about the antibiotics. "I'm sorry. I was sick. I

should have remembered. I was so busy with work, though. When I started throwing up, I thought it was still the flu, and then...then I realized what had happened, and..."

"How long have you known?"

"Four days," I whisper. Zeth doesn't move. I wish he would. I wish he would pick something up. Throw something. I wish he would speak. Shout. Laugh. Cry. *Anything*. I need to know what he's thinking. Either way, good or bad, I just want to know, so we can deal with it. He just stands there, staring, though. The muscles in his arms keep twitching, the tattoos marking his skin shifting as he fights to figure out how to stop his body from trembling.

"Zeth—"

He turns around quickly, picks up his leather jacket from the coat rack, and then he storms out of the house, slamming the door behind him. The house rings with the sound, echoing like a shotgun.

Oh shit. Fuck, shit, fuck.

I lean forward, bracing myself against my knees, trying to slow down the frantic racing of my heart. Now I really can't breathe. I can't even form a coherent thought.

He—he didn't—he didn't even say anything. How? How could he just leave without breathing one word to calm me, to make me feel better? How could he have stood there for all of those drawn out seconds and be able to hide his reaction so well? He's angry. He's angry and he hates me for this, I just know it. God, I can't fucking breathe. I can't fucking—

The door swings open again, ripped open so violently that it's a miracle it remains attached to its hinges. Zeth storms back into the house like a force of nature, a whirlwind, unstoppable, charged and snapping with energy. He throws his jacket onto the ground, coming to a stop three feet away from me.

"You're *pregnant,*" he says, running his hands through his hair. It's a statement this time, not a question. "You are pregnant. With a baby. With *my* baby."

"Yes." He's not implying that I've been sleeping with someone else, and there's a chance it's not his. I can tell by the stunned look on his face that he's just trying to get his head around the concept. I've had a couple of days to let this news settle in, after all, and it still has me reeling. It's understandable that he's so stunned.

"This...I wasn't expecting this," he says. "We never spoke about children, Sloane."

"I know. It was a shock to me too, believe me."

"How far along are you?"

"Not long. Only three weeks."

He nods. Nods, and then starts pacing up and down. His fingers are still buried deep in his hair. "And...you..." He blows out a deep breath. Shakes his head. Growls under his breath. I've never seen him like this. He doesn't know what to say. How to say it. I can already hear the words, though.

I put him out of his misery and voice them myself. "And I want to keep it?"

He freezes, eyes locking onto mine. The tips of his ears are bright red. "I know you're not going to get rid of it, Sloane. I just want to know if..." He scowls, clenching his hands into fists. Frustrated isn't the word for his emotional state right now. It's something bigger, something more than that, but I just can't seem to put a name to it. He sinks into the armchair opposite me, his head hanging, chin almost touching his chest. He looks defeated.

"I want to know how you feel about it," he says, rushing the words out. "I want to know if having a baby, having *my* baby, is something you think will make you...*happy*. Can you...can you see it? In your head?"

He's never looked more vulnerable. God, I want to rush across the room and throw myself at him, but Zeth handles his feelings in strange ways. He won't be able to cope with me mothering him. He'll reject it. He needs me to give him time to get his words out, and he needs me to answer him as plainly and simply as I can. So I do.

"Yes. Yes, I can see it. I can see it all. I want this baby. He's half of me and half of you. How can I not want that? I was scared to even think about it for a while, I'll admit it, but I *know* now. This isn't planned, and the timing sure as hell isn't right, but I know we can make it work. If you're here with me, we can do anything."

He sits very still, digesting my words. His head is still hanging, like he's bracing for the worst news of his life. Maybe this is it. I could seriously just have delivered the most terrible news Zeth Mayfair will ever receive. God, I hope I haven't. I'm praying that's not the case when he lifts his head and I see the tears in his eyes.

"Thank god," he whispers.

A wave crashes into me, so strong and powerful that I can feel the relief reaching down and taking hold of me, so intense that my head spins. I let out a choked sob and then clamp my hands over my mouth, trying to hold back the other, louder sobs that are building in my chest. Zeth jumps up out of his chair and rushes to me, taking hold of me and lifting me off the sofa into his arms.

"I can't believe it," he says, whispering into my hair. "Don't cry, angry girl. Everything's going to be okay. Everything's going to be okay, I promise. I *swear* to you. Fuck, I love you so much."

I cling to him, barely keeping my shit together. Ahh, who am I kidding? I don't keep my shit together at all. I cry until his t-shirt is soaked with a patch of my tears, and my throat is aching so badly that it hurts to swallow. I was too afraid to even let myself imagine that he might take this news well, so the fact that he's comforting me, telling me everything's going to be all right, that he loves me, makes me feel like my heart is overflowing.

"Can *you* see it?" I ask. "Can you see us having a family? Do you think it will make *you* happy?"

Zeth lets out a shaky breath. He presses his forehead against mine, closing his eyes. "I'm already happy, Sloane. I don't deserve you, and I don't deserve this baby. It's a fucking miracle. The most precious fucking gift. I don't...I just don't want to fuck it up."

I cup the side of his face in my hand. How did the stars align so that I would meet this man? Both of us have walked such very different paths, our lives guiding us in such different directions, our pain and our suffering carving us into two vastly different creatures, and yet somehow fate brought us together. We found that our differences brought us closer to one another, and our pasts held no power over the future we might share if we wanted it.

And now, a baby. *Our baby.* Still such a strange, alien thought, and yet I feel like another piece of our puzzle has snapped into place, revealing a little more of the story of our lives together. Who knows how many more pieces there are yet to be revealed. Who knows what the end picture will look like. All I know is that this man holding me in his arms is raw, and dangerous, and volatile, and he is fierce, and protective, and kind at the same time.

"You're not going to fuck it up," I tell him. "You're gonna knock this out of the park, Zeth Mayfair."

He kisses me like a man drowning, then, crushing his lips against mine as if I'm his oxygen, I'm his life force, and he just can't get enough. I kiss him back, clinging to him, unable to get close enough. When he cuts the kiss short, I take the opportunity to ask him one more time. "Please don't go to New York, Zeth. *Please*. I need you here, with me. *Alive*."

He looks conflicted, his eyes flickering with anger. "I'll stay. I'm not going anywhere now. But, shit, Sloane. This thing's going to come to a head one way or another. I'm going to be ready. It's not just you I have to think about now."

He's right, naturally. The warehouse burning down isn't going to be an isolated event. When it comes to money and power, men and women alike transform into people entirely unlike themselves. It's an addiction, and just like any form of addiction, the addict will do anything and everything they can to feed their vice.

The Italians will be back. The prospect is a frightening one, almost too frightening to think about right now, but if there's one thing I'm sure of, it's that Zeth will be true to his word. He'll keep us safe. He won't let anything happen to us.

I feel stupid for having waited so long to tell him. Michael was right; I should have trusted him. I feel weightless as Zeth carries me upstairs to our bedroom. I'm sure now that having this baby won't break us.

Quite the opposite. In fact, strange though it might seem, I believe that having this baby might just end up being our salvation.

ACKNOWLEDGEMENTS

Firstly, a confession: I am not a doctor. I love writing about Sloane's work, and I do my best to make sure everything is as accurate as possible. When it comes to patients' conditions and the medication administered to them, I always really try to ensure the veracity of the information I include, but sometimes a lay person's understanding of human biology and medicine means that errors might occur. I apologize in advance if any such mistakes have occurred within the pages of this novel, and I humbly ask for your forgiveness.

Secondly, another confession: I am an English! I live in the states now, and I do write using American English. My books are all edited to check that the content is geared in that direction, however sometimes my English brain will speed way ahead of me, things might get missed, and grammar and spelling might be anglicised. If this happens and you see a rogue U or S in a word, or you're not 100% familiar with a particular turn of phrase, rest assured that I'm not illiterate and it's simply my Blighty roots shining through. Again, please forgive!

Now we get down to the good stuff. The thanking part.

In no particular order of favourites (see what I did there?), huge thanks must go to Tyler Chesser, Kirsten Stomberg Bumpus, Alice Kulbat, and Jessica Roscoe for cheering me on with this project and keeping me writing. Jess's alter ego, Lili Saint Germain, must definitely be thanked for sprinting with me, so that I managed to get words down on paper while I was on the road.

Thanks to Fiona Wilson for the fast, efficient editing. Thanks to Rebecca Shea for the Starbucks coconut macchiato suggestion—that shit kept me going more than you will ever know! Thanks to Gemma Curran, Kylie Sharp and Emma Keating for the continued support you show me every time I write a new book. I am endlessly grateful for the time and energy you put into helping me.

Gemma Sherlock, thank you for signing up to help me muddle through this whole crazy author gig. Your assistance means I get to do what I love most: write.

Lastly, thank you to you, Dear Reader, for continuing to follow Zeth & Sloane's story and to invest in their rocky, romantic, crazy, adventure filled lives together. It's very easy as an author to forget sometimes that the people you write about every day aren't, in actual fact, real, and to know that you guys have gotten as lost as I have in this journey is the most rewarding thing in the world.

Thank you

X

CALLIE'S NEWSLETTER
LOTTERY

As a token of her appreciation for reading and supporting her work, at the end of every month, Callie and her team will be hosting a HUGE giveaway with a mass of goodies up for grabs, including vouchers, e-readers, signed books, signed swag, author event tickets and exclusive paperback copies of stories no one else in the world will have access to!

All you need to do to automatically enter each month is be signed up to her newsletter, which you can do right here:

http://eepurl.com/IzhzL

ABOUT THE AUTHOR

Callie Hart is the author of the international bestselling Blood & Roses Series. She considers herself a true citizen of the world, having lived and traveled in many different countries. Her passion for writing can only be topped by her love for reading. When she's not buried in a book, you can find her lost in Game of Thrones or some other fantastical world.

••••

If you want to know the second one of Callie's books goes live, all you need to do is sign up here.

http://eepurl.com/IzhzL

CALLIE WANTS TO HEAR FROM YOU!

To visit Callie's **website**, head to
http://calliehart.com

Find Callie on her **Facebook Page** , at
http://www.facebook.com/calliehartauthor

or her **Facebook Profile**
http://www.facebook.com/callie.hart.777

Blog
http://calliehart.blogspot.com.au

Twitter
http://www.twitter.com/_callie_hart

Goodreads
http://www.goodreads.com/author/show/
7771953.Callie_Hart

To sign up for her **newsletter**, head over to
http://eepurl.com/IzhzL

TELL ME YOUR FAVORITE BIT!

Don't forget!

If you purchased Savage Things and loved it, then please do stop over to your online retailer of choice and let me know which were your favorite parts!

Reading reviews is the highlight of any author's day.

I must ask, though...if you do review Savage Things, please do your best to keep it spoiler free or indicate your spoilers clearly. There's nothing worse than purchasing a book only to accidentally ruin the twists and turns by reading something by accident!

Made in the USA
Middletown, DE
30 January 2023